DON JADU

SEK Mqhayi

Translated from isiXhosa by Thokozile Mabeqa,
Nosisi Mpolweni and Thenjiswa Ntwana

OXFORD
UNIVERSITY PRESS

SOUTH AFRICA

OXFORD
UNIVERSITY PRESS

Oxford University Press is a department of the University of Oxford.
It furthers the University's objective of excellence in research, scholarship,
and education by publishing worldwide. Oxford is a registered trade mark of
Oxford University Press in the UK and in certain other countries.

Published in South Africa by
Oxford University Press Southern Africa (Pty) Limited

Vasco Boulevard, Goodwood, N1 City, P O Box 12119, Cape Town,
South Africa

Don Jadu

ISBN 978 0 19 073708 5 (print)
ISBN 978 0 19 075088 6 (ebook)

First impression 2018

Typeset in Utopia Std 10.5pt on 15.5pt
Printed on 70gsm woodfree paper

Acknowledgements
Co-ordinator at the Centre for Multilingualism and Diversities Research, UWC: Antjie Krog
Publisher: Helga Schaberg
Project manager: Liz Sparg
Editor: Mary Reynolds
Book and cover designer: Judith Cross
Typesetter: Aptara Inc.
Printed and bound by: Academic Press

We are grateful to the following for permission to reproduce photographs: Shutterstock/
Diego Cervo/106684193 (cover); South African National Library, Cape Town (pp. iv, 2);
CMDR (photo of Thokozile Mabeqa p. 107); Thenjiswa Ntwana (p. 107); OUPSA/Admire
Kanhenga (p. 108)

The authors and publisher gratefully acknowledge permission to reproduce copyright
material in this book. Every effort has been made to trace copyright holders, but if any
copyright infringements have been made, the publisher would be grateful for information
that would enable any omissions or errors to be corrected in subsequent impressions.

Links to third party websites are provided by Oxford in good faith and for information only.
Oxford disclaims any responsibility for the materials contained in any third party website
referenced in this work.

THIS BOOK FORMS part of a series of eight texts and a larger translation endeavour undertaken by the Centre for Multilingualism and Diversities Research (CMDR) at the University of the Western Cape (UWC). The texts translated for this series have been identified time and again by scholars of literature in southern Africa as classics in their original languages. The translators were selected for their translation experience and knowledge of a particular indigenous language. Funding was provided by the National Institute for the Humanities and Social Sciences (NIHSS) as part of their Catalytic Research Programme. The project seeks to stimulate debate by inserting neglected or previously untranslated literary texts into contemporary public spheres, providing opportunities to refigure their significance and prompting epistemic changes within multidisciplinary research. Every generation translates for itself. Within the broad scope of several translation theories and the fact that every person translates differently from the next, it is hoped that these texts will generate further deliberations, translations and retranslations.

NATIONAL INSTITUTE
FOR THE HUMANITIES
AND SOCIAL SCIENCES

UNIVERSITY *of the*
WESTERN CAPE

Centre for Multilingualism
and Diversities Research

SEK Mqhayi (1875–1945)

SEK Mqhayi is often referred to as imbongi yesizwe jikelele (the poet of the nation) and was called the "poet laureate of the African people" by the young Nelson Mandela. He was born in 1875 in Gqumashe, a village in the Eastern Cape. In his youth, he spent six years living in Centane, and the knowledge of the language and customs of the Xhosa that he gained while living there had a great impact on his life and his future writing. He was a prolific contributor to newspapers, including the influential *Izwi Labantu*, which he also edited. Mqhayi rapidly became a towering figure in isiXhosa literature. He was the first imbongi to write down his poetry and it is said that his contribution to making new words in his novels fills many pages in isiXhosa dictionaries. His first novel – an adaptation of the biblical story of Samson – was written in 1907, but has been lost. This was followed by *Ityala Lamawele* (The lawsuit of the twins) and *UDon Jadu* (Don Jadu), which have both become classics in isiXhosa literature. *UDon Jadu* ushered in a more "socially rather than simply morally grounded understanding of the various forms of alienation that blacks were experiencing in the cities … Since there is no pristine 'homeland' to retreat to (given the instances of serfdom that Don Jadu witnesses), Mqhayi imagines a future utopian, non-racial and egalitarian society, where there is respect and work for everyone: a place that he tellingly calls *Mnandi*, that is, bliss or sweetness" (Bhekizizwe Peterson, *The Cambridge History of South African Literature*, page 305).

Mqhayi added several stanzas to Enoch Sontonga's hymn "Nkosi Sikelel' iAfrika", now South Africa's national anthem. He also published his first published collection of poems in isiXhosa: *Imihobe Nemibongo* (Songs of joy and lullabies) in 1927, an autobiography, *U-Mqhayi wase Ntab'ozuko* (Mqhayi of the Mount of Glory) in 1939 and another poetry volume *Inzuzo* (Reward) in 1942. He twice won the May Esther Bedford Prize for Bantu literature.

Don Jadu: The long road to freedom

By the end of the nineteenth century South Africa was changing very fast: Britain had broken the power of the African monarchies and handed colonial control to the Boer and British settlers in a union that recognised only the rights of white people. Diamonds and gold had been discovered and the mines needed large numbers of workers. Laws, taxes and the 1913 Natives Land Act forced people off the land, causing overcrowding, land hunger, poverty and starvation. By the 1920s government policies had become harsher and more racist. But by 1921, following the emergence of liberation movements, several organisations including the International Socialist League had merged to form the Communist Party of South Africa, and so created a broader context of race and class.

In an unprecedented feat of the imagination, Mqhayi wrote this visionary allegory while the world around him was swirling with violence and turmoil caused by various world views clashing within destructive colonial encounters.

He imagines an ideal state, which in many ways is a vision predicting what was to come in South Africa only towards the end of the twentieth century. Mqhayi – a traditional Xhosa imbongi, a writer, journalist, historian and politician among many things – kept his eye on the future, sometimes so far into the future that his peers began to doubt his rationality as they battled to comprehend him. As I have indicated elsewhere (in "Images in Some of the Literary Works of SEK Mqhayi"), *Don Jadu* was denounced by earlier critics as incongruous and thus inconsequential, but was later acclaimed as one of the books in which Mqhayi exhibits artistry of a rare quality.

Indeed, as history progressed, it was this close resemblance between *Don Jadu* and a changing South Africa that moved Sirayi (1989: 111) to observe that, among other things, Mqhayi is visualising "African society undergoing socio-political change". Furthermore, when, far ahead of his time, Mqhayi implored the powers that be to work towards creating a South Africa in which all people would enjoy equal rights irrespective of colour, creed and nationality, he was planting seeds with his prophetic images.

Don Jadu tells the story of a young man's journey to visit his aunt. Small, seemingly innocent and often quite funny things happen involving encounters with people, ostriches, a puff adder, dogs and so forth, all of which prompt the reflective narrator to draw parallels with human nature. After a number of years this young man journeys this same route again, but this time to investigate the possibility of establishing a space in which black people can rule themselves. On the palimpsest of the first two journeys, the story of a third one takes place, in which he recounts the success of this endeavour to create an ideal state.

On each of these journeys, the writer uses his main character, Don Jadu, as both "an interpreter of what is happening and a guide as to how to respond" (Schoots 2014: 48). Jonathan Schoots (2014: 71) describes the kind of ideal state Mqhayi portrays as presenting a "fascinating vision of modernity and hybridity where Christian and traditional Xhosa rituals are blended together and where there is restorative justice and broad social equality."

In "The Sociological Imagination of SEK Mqhayi: Towards an African Sociology" Schoots (2014: 48) says the following about Mqhayi's writing:

> His work is all the more powerful because he is able to maintain coherence within the 'Xhosa world view'– reinterpreting it and using its metaphors and 'common sense' knowledge to interpret the new world. By drawing on concepts that already exist as 'given' or 'taken for granted' in the Xhosa knowledge system he is able to make the new

world intelligible by people who inhabit the 'old world'. It is this ability to explain the new as a continuation of an older tradition that makes Mqhayi's work so powerful and explains why he has been so revered as a public figure in his own time and why his work is still drawn on today.

Scholars often force binary choices into the work of Mqhayi, but it is precisely his ability to draw on his own culture, change in it what he does not find useful, and weave into it whatever he does find useful from other cultures that brings the visionary quality that is always present in whatever he is writing.

Mqhayi was envisaging democracy long before it was a reality. As a prelude to *Don Jadu*, he published an essay in *Umteteli wa Bantu* in 1923, in which the intellectual content of the *Don Jadu* story was already neatly formulated. He included the following:

- *Zesithi sakukhululeka kwingcinezelo yegwangqa* – liberation from colonial rule and oppression, followed by political freedom and democracy
- *Kuchithwe iintlanti ngamadoda kumiswe ezintsha* – total departure from traditional socio-economic practices to modern scientific socio-economic systems
- *Kumiswe amatye ezikhumbuzo zabo bazenza idini bafela emadabini* – construction of memorial monuments for those who sacrificed their lives fighting and dying in battles for the many to live
- *Kuvuselelwe izikumkani, kwakhiwe isizwe, kugcinwe umthetho, kulondolozwe amasiko nezithethe* – restoration and revival of the legacy of kings, preservation of culture, upholding and respecting the rule of law

Certainly whoever read those words in 1923 could never have thought that the first line *"Zesithi sakukhululeka kwingcinezelo yegwangqa"* (referring to when there would be liberation from oppression by the white man), would come true in 1990, when Nelson Mandela walked out of Pollsmoor prison to create a democratic dispensation. Mqhayi would have stood up in his grave if he had been able to hear that what he had foretold in the early twentieth century had become reality a century later.

Mqhayi's traveller and subsequent leader, Don Jadu, is adamant that no nationality can regard itself as superior to others. With Christianity and education as guides, and with the strength of social cohesion, Don Jadu views *all* the people of the country as a community progressively committed to a future in the contemporary world under the decisive leadership of black people.

Mqhayi did for isiXhosa what Shakespeare did for English, and what brilliant writers throughout world history should, in Ngũgĩ' wa Thiongo's view, be doing for their languages: "meeting the challenge of creating a literature in them, which process later opens the languages for philosophy, science, technology and all the other areas of human creative endeavours" ([1981] 2005: 29).

There is no better time than the present to read *Don Jadu*, as South African society attempts to restructure itself and regain lost values, as it must before it can successfully and rationally live as a caring nation in today's complex world.

Professor Ncedile Saule
Alice, Eastern Cape
May 2018

References

Mqhayi, SEK (1923) "Imfuduko enkulu" in *Umteteli wa Bantu,*
    9 July, page 7.
Saule, N (1996) *Images in Some of the Literary Works of SEK Mqhayi*
    (PhD thesis). University of South Africa, Pretoria.

Schoots, J (2014) *The Sociological Imagination of SEK Mqhayi: Towards an African Sociology* (MPhil thesis). University of Cape Town.

Sirayi, GT (1989) *The Xhosa Novel* (DLitt and Phil thesis). University of South Africa, Pretoria.

wa Thiong'o, Ngũgĩ ([1981]2005) *Decolonising the Mind: The Politics of Language in African Literature*. Oxford: James Currey; Nairobi: East African Educational Publishers; Portsmouth, USA: Heinemann.

DON JADU

TRAVELLING IS EDUCATION

A story that encourages unity
and development

SEK Mqhayi

The national poet: This is the Xhosa poet who sang praises to the Prince of Wales.

Cape Times, 29 May 1925

Preface

The narrator of this novelette is the Honourable Dondolo, son of Jadu of the Zima clan, but to shorten it he calls himself Don Jadu.

In relating this story he says:

> "I leave it up to each and every one
> To believe it, if he believes;
> To dismiss it, if he doesn't believe it,
> I won't blame anyone."

Although the honourable narrator was born during this period of modern progress and civilisation, he grew up in the rural areas of Xhosaland. He is well educated; he has even received qualifications from overseas and the Far East.

I will end here and leave it to Dondolo to tell his own story. Yours today and yesterday,

SE Krune Mqhayi
Ntab'ozuko
Berlin, Cape Province
February 1929

Contents

SECTION ONE

1

The spark

Once, when I was still a young man of twenty years old, I left home in the Xhosa rural areas and went to one of the towns. It so happened that one day, while still in town, I thought of going to see my aunt, my grandfather's daughter who had got married back at home where I lived, but due to the scatterings, had moved to a semi-urban area, a place of the Rhanuga people[1], the displaced, the bastardised. The distance from the town to her home was just over thirty miles.

The police. – As soon as it struck my mind that I should pay her a visit, I hastened, but the moment I gave the town my back at the exit, I came across two policemen, the one behind the other, riding their geldings – in front was a white policeman, at the back was a black one. As soon as the white policeman approached me, he asked for my dompas, as an identity book was called. I answered in isiXhosa, "I have never carried that thing." Now he pumped me with questions: "Why? Why not? What nationality are you? Are you a Lawu?" I said, "I'm a Jingqi[2], an indigenous citizen." Hearing these words, this one of ours who was black, jumped like lightning from his horse and charged me, "How dare you! You think you can break the law, because of your claim to be a Jingqi? Who do you think you are!" He walked up to me with handcuffs, but I pushed him away: "Let go of me, don't vomit on us!" After I said that, the white policeman turned away (I truly don't know what he had learnt from this remark) and continued his journey, saying: "Let him go!" and my fellow man immediately backed off, grumbling, of which I could only hear the following: "Nokhala, my ancestors, I've never had that kind of challenge from a mere Xhosa."

At last I could start on my own journey, pondering this disgusting confrontation with my own fellow man. I tried to remind myself that his life and that of his family depended on this kind of behaviour; without presenting an aggressive stance he could not get any promotion nor trust from his employer. I was left with self-pity for the nation to which I belong, because although today I suddenly found myself a stranger, my rescue should have come from him, my shelter should have been this very person who wanted me to end up in a dungeon simply because he was doing what provided bread for him; if he did not use a hostile approach, he would not be advanced. What I found worse was that he executed his orders so wholeheartedly; even the law that I supposedly broke – my failure to produce identification – seemed as though it was his own law; so the root cause of his behaviour was the protection of his own living ones. This confirmed the saying: "Never lean on a man with an empty stomach." I was also thinking: do you know what, there was absolutely no dispute between me and this fellow man, no fighting, but in our first encounter this was how we treated one another, just like dogs.

The robbers. – Now I had been travelling through a thick, dark forest that stretched alongside a river valley; this was a notorious place, but I had never paid attention to the rumours about it. Just before I approached the most impenetrable part, I immediately sensed danger and, indeed, barely halfway through, there came a kind of breaking, crackling sound, "Tywakakaba-tywaba" from the thick bush – and I heard a voice: "Tobacco please!" I tried to ignore it but the man persisted, "Fellow man, I say, tobacco please! Are you deaf?" I responded immediately, "I have no tobacco." "What! How dare you talk to me like that, fellow man? Who do you think you are?" said the voice coming out of the forest. I said, "Oh! Then come and take it, in the same way that you usually take from people."

Just as I was uttering these words, I took a sharp look in front of me – what was this! There stood the robbers, ready for action: one of them a Lawu man, and the two behind him were fellows I would classify as murderous robbers. Oh! Realising that I was in trouble, I was heard to say, appealing to both sides: "You know what, gentlemen, the job we are about to embark on is important, because there will be one or two of you that I will leave lying on the ground – I therefore ask you to write down your last wish, and I will do the same – I will write my own will and testament." As I was saying these words, putting my bag down as though I was about to take out some paper – awu! – for a reason unknown to me, I suddenly heard the frantic footsteps of the Lawu as if he had fallen from a rooftop, running very fast, grabbing at his waist, yelling: "He is taking out a pistol, guys! Watch out! Watch out!" In a split second, all the men just vanished into thin air; even when I shouted: "He is lying, I have no pistol!" But it was as though I had blown them away – they just disappeared. I was left standing alone at that spot thinking about the saying "sinners run unchased", but then my thoughts returned to my journey as there was still a long road ahead. Eventually I left. While travelling along, I thought about this habit of our fellow men who thirst so vigorously for the blood of their own that they skulk in dark forests in search of it, and I was struck dumb.

What made a particular impression on my mind was the fact that such grown-up men could be misled by a Lawu, lying to them so convincingly, whereas they could have benefited greatly by staying and robbing. Actually, I had no pistol, nor any sharp weapon at all; the only thing I had with me was a smooth blemishless knobkierie; that is what I was taught to carry and use when I was among other men. I say these robbers could have benefited a lot because these men often wasted so much energy robbing a person to death for a mere shilling which they then would share among themselves, as well as the rags that their victim was wearing. But my case could have been different because I had ten pounds with me; even the value of my clothes amounted to ten pounds, including the bag packed with more clothes plus the umbrella; all of these I was using for the first time.

My thoughts about this incident with the robbers made me realise that, you know what? Our people are like this all over the world; you may find men gathering together, sharing an idea until they reach a productive agreement that will benefit them all – but just when things materialise, there comes a minuscule Lawu who destroys that unity, scattering the members. If these gentlemen had been determined to kill me and had ignored everything I said but simply attacked me with full force, they would have achieved their mission and found something to take back to their families, no matter how small. But now they had been frightened away by the lies and cowardice of a Lawu man. Why is it that our people have a tendency to involve outsiders when they are doing things, instead of doing what they want to do independently? Do you know what? An outsider simply disrupts unity and leads people astray.

2

Other challenges

The ostriches. – Eventually I came out of the dense forest, crossed a hill and then approached a stretched-out open plain – but saw it was crowded with brown and black ostriches. Now you have to understand that we who have grown up in the land of the Xhosa, we don't take ostriches lightly. We never played near an ostrich because we didn't know them – we were scared, especially of a female ostrich, and even of those that were said to be unable to kick – we didn't want them to learn on us because we had no knowledge of the tricks needed to fight them.

I could be seen stopping, pausing to figure out a strategy to skirt this horde of ostriches. I decided on a detour to the right so that the bulk of them should be on my left; I also noticed that beyond this crowd there was a wire fence spanning the plain, which could intervene on my behalf if I could get there. If my journey could lead me successfully to the fence, there was a gate – however, reaching that gate was in itself a problem as it could be regarded as yet another trespass.

Eventually I left the road and walked down a slope through thick grass and thorn trees until I reached a small stream, and I crossed where there was no bridge, jumping over dongas and shrubs that stretched everywhere; finally, I cleared the stream and realised that if it was not for the protection of my shoes and clothes, my feet and calves would have been victims of the thorns. With gusto I walked through that stretch of land, here and there dodging clusters of ostriches; some of them simply opened their beaks – those beaks that I did not like – while others shook their wings but left me to continue my journey unharmed. By this time I was already tired, when I suddenly noticed two black shiny things with red shins fighting, truly, a very fierce ugly fight! The way in which the feathers fell was like a hailstorm! I stealthily slipped past – but at that moment of quietly dashing by, both of them spotted me and immediately forgot whatever business they had not agreed upon and chased the stranger – who was I. The speed of an ostrich is also described in the Bible: "An ostrich just laughs at the horse and its owner." Oh yes! I quickly realised there was only one plan at this point, to beg my calves to do the work they were supposed to do. To run fast was not what I was known for, but I drew on even the last little dregs of breath, and beyond that came out with whatever secret reserves I had in me that I didn't know I had.

While running as fast as I could, my first hope was that my enemies would at least be worn out from their fierce fighting, and therefore would not be as fast as they usually were; my other hope was that they had only seen me when I was already some distance away, and I was now close to the fence I had seen beyond the ostriches. But my hopes were short-lived.

I have already mentioned that age-wise, I was in my twenties; my height was nearly six foot (5 foot 9 inches). My weight, measured on that very morning, was two hundred and five pounds (205 lb); so you will understand that this weight is not aligned to my age, and it is definitely not a weight that can assist someone to move more sweetly.

It seemed like a joke when shortness of breath attacked me; at the same time that the ostriches were catching up behind me, I ran and moved on, moved on and ran until the fence was only a hundred and one yards away, desperately pushing on, running, moving on until the fence was at last eleven yards away, but by then, I could already feel the breath of the footsteps of the ostriches, with their wings flying in the air behind me. By this time all of us were running chaotically to the fence, and there was no time to open the gate – I just threw myself at the fence and since it was barbed wire, got what I deserved; but barely halfway through the fence, I heard the frightening sound of a giant ostrich at my back: "Xwa!", with the rest of the ostriches following with an overwhelming noise, and it was as though the pillars of the fence were uprooted. The giant ostrich threw itself at the fence and squashed itself into a ball.

I narrowly escaped, then threw myself onto mpepho shrubs and some ragwort, sprawling helplessly. Meanwhile, the two ostriches were now standing right in front of me, brushing each other with their beaks. This act of the two ostriches made me think deeply: just a few seconds before, these two were fighting viciously but when they saw a common enemy, they set aside their squabbles and differences and chased the stranger. I realised that they were teaching a lesson to me in particular, and to my fellow men: we people, who cannot set aside our differences and focus on the common enemy facing us. The result is that we remain easy prey to our enemies, we pitch fights against one another, and destroy ourselves into nonentities; we become undone. I began to admire these ostriches for the wisdom I found in them, which surpassed mine and even that of my nation.

The puff adder. – While lying exhausted on this patch of grass and shrubs, thinking about all these things, I felt something moving underneath me with a puffing sound, but did not immediately take notice, my mind still stolen by the ostriches. When I came to my senses, I jumped up and looked. "Awu! What is happening now? Does this journey have no blessings?" Clearly, in that patch onto which I had thrown myself with such abandon was a big puff adder. The snake looked like part of a rocky outcrop and was the colour of an old weathered white shirt – it was the kind of puff adder that has as much venom as a brown tree snake, because it shares the same habitat and diet; one bite from this snake secures death. Now, after I had spotted it, I leapt up as fast as though I had been blasted by dynamite. In truth, I cannot describe how I got up; but as a result of my superior jump, the ostriches scattered in all directions over the veld, now being surprised by me, the one whom they had been chasing, exclaiming: "How dare you!" This incident taught me that you cannot always win: there comes a time when you must expect to lose. A hero who insists on heroism every day dies young, becomes green, without being of value to his nation nor to anyone else.

I then thrashed that snake until I had made sure that I fulfilled the saying, "The descendants of a woman will crush the head of the snake's descendants." My mind came back to me from the ostriches and focused on the incident with the snake. I asked myself: how on earth did it leave me unharmed? Why did it simply fume and puff before it could bite me? Maybe the fuming was the snake praising itself, but why would it praise itself before accomplishing the job it was already boasting of? I found this snake an under-performer just as I myself and my people were, because we praised each other, even for disgusting acts, or for having done nothing. To my mind, this puff adder could have just kept silent and quietly found the right moment to attack me and only then start to praise itself so that by the time it died, it would have accomplished the duty of its nation: crushing the heel of the nation that was stepping on it.

The Boers. – Just when I was still churning these incidents over in my head, preparing to get back to my journey, I heard a sound quite close behind me – fu-fu-fu-fu! When I turned around, it was trouble! A cloud of dust! Unknown, terrifying sounds! Language I didn't know! A hail of insults! The lashing of sjamboks! You name it – what now? Then I faintly heard: "Empty-headed cripple! Slow-witted baboon! Stupid kaffir!" What was this? What had happened now? There was a lot I didn't understand, but I was sure I was not hearing a praise poem. Was there time to ask something, I wondered, while being grabbed and dragged like an ox to be slaughtered: why all this now? It was the Boers, the owners of the farm that I was passing through; I thought I was escaping the ostriches, only to find I had thrown myself into a furnace!

What had happened was that I had come across two Boers riding two big, well-built horses, geldings! They took me to the middle of the road and told me that I would be going back, heading for the jail in the same town that I had left that morning! The opportunity to plead on my own behalf was scarcer than anything else in the world. Should I try to open my mouth to say, "Baas!" – Oh no! No matter how short this word was, the sjambok would bite me before I had finished saying it.

And suddenly even the clothes I wore seemed to be an offence, and the beautiful bag I was carrying started to look dirty. I now began to feel it would have been better to have been arrested by the police who I had met in the morning, because at least then I was still close to town. The spirit of bravery that I had felt then had vanished, and I found myself a tame lamb. I reflected on my fearlessness when I was confronted by the police that morning and by those robbers. So why was I now scared – especially when I could see that one of these two men did not have much muscle, even though the other one was a hefty bearded Boer? These thoughts remained mere thoughts, but the truth was: I was terrified of these men!

I just followed their instructions: off they dragged me to the gate in the fence, escorting me with insults, and mocking and hounding me to the extent that the horses nearly trampled my heels!

When I arrived at the gate, another thought came to mind: I should not bother so much about these acts: there was my Owner, even I am not mine; I am nothing without Him; after this thought, anxiety lifted from my chest and I was at peace! I found myself talking to myself: "He is mine and I am His." I heard the two asking each other what I was saying; and they replied to each other that they had no clue and began laughing their lungs out.

Just at that moment, another Boer came along! He was galloping, and on arrival lifted his arm as though to strike, threatening me with a sjambok, shouting and insulting me just like the policemen had! Apparently, he was the father of the other two, an elderly man who would have looked better if he wasn't in this country – a man with a beard down to his stomach. Just in the midst of this confrontation, he said in his language, "Yes, my *kameraad*, what are you saying now?" He uttered these words standing right in front of me, as if he was about to push his horse onto me while beating me simultaneously with the sjambok on the back.

While we were looking at each other, the Boer and myself, suddenly here his whole family was: people of all kinds, boys, girls, little thin-legged ones with crust in their eyes as if they had just woken up, grovelling snot-nosed ones – with flies going bu-u-u! The servants were also there, wearing nothing besides sacks, with holes for their arms. This whole group was gathering around me, laughing under their breath, ganging up against me, giggling, laughing, and having fun!

While we were eyeing one another, not in a pleasant manner, something said to me, "Just look over there." I responded, and saw a long line of black people carrying their bags of food slung over their shoulders, with black-and-white containers used for boiling water. Right then, it struck my mind that I should make something of this circumstance so that it might save me, because one manages to escape by swerving this way and that; and the nature of my journey had already taught me this.

So what did I do? Immediately I brightened up, joyfully cried out, and beckoning them, hastened to welcome them: "Help! Come near, you Lawu people!" They replied but I could not make out what they were saying; however, their response alone offered untold help to me, and soon they turned back and came towards me, not in slow motion.

What is he saying? I heard one of the Boers saying: "Jere Got!" and those were their last words: the horses kicked dust, the father leading the way. Whether they left to get some help, or where they went to, didn't interest me at all. So what happened to the family and servants of the Boer? And also their dogs and everything else? You still ask? Why wouldn't they lift their shins, following their fathers and masters? I didn't care to look at them thronging away.

Apparently, the group of people that I had spoken to were coming from the gold mines in Johannesburg. As soon as we were alone, they related the hard experiences from where they were coming. I did not have much to say, just found myself stunned, and said: "I don't know men who are like those Boers." As I was uttering these shocked words, these men exclaimed loudly: "Awu! Do these Boers still have those bad habits?" They related in detail a variety of bad habits these Boers had, until it became clear to me that they knew them well, so I then asked how they knew them. "We grew up together – our families lived on the farms, they are still up there, beyond that ridge that you crossed."

I did not want to ask anything further; they also did not pose any more questions, and they were satisfied with what they knew. I felt I had to say something, express my words of thanks to them, but there were no words, my voice was burnt. I only heard this tiny little voice coming out, saying: "The kind gesture that you have bestowed on me will soon be rewarded."

I then abruptly left, deeply moved, as if hit by the wind, and went on my way, leaving them sitting in the shade, making a fire to prepare something to eat as they were also close to a source of water. It seemed as if they would have liked me to join them for the meal, and to tell the truth, I was starving, but by this time, I was preoccupied with a bad feeling.

Hungry as I was, I managed to cover quite a long distance, meditating on words that come from a song in the hymn-book: "He is mine and I am His." Just at that moment, can you believe it, I came across another hefty Boer. He said: "Ah! You managed to escape from those robbers." I just kept quiet, looked at him, and did not utter a word; not because I was scared this time, I was just amazed by the way someone who was not a mother tongue speaker of our language could speak it so fluently; secondly, I was wondering where he was when I was confronted by the robbers.

This Boer concluded: "You know what, you put your life in danger through stupidity. There's a house not far from here, and the route to that house goes right past my home. That homestead has escorts that accompany visitors until they pass this gate, to save visitors from the ostriches and those robbers!" I did not utter a word, but had a lot of questions in my mind; also about him, yes, him: to me there seemed to be a group of robbers of which he was one. I just stood up and resumed my journey.

When I was myself again, I recalled the behaviour of all those Boers, but my thoughts refused to push ahead and go forward; there was no space for further analysis. My thoughts kept hitting against the question: "What kind of human treats a stranger like this?" I ended up concluding that our Lord knew exactly what kind of ubuntu the people from outside, the foreigners, had, and that was why He had said: "I was a stranger, and you did not welcome me in your home."

By this time, the sun was above me and the heat unbearable, so I took off my jacket and hung it on one shoulder and walked on. It was then that I saw – Oh, no! Can you believe it? The large fang of a puff adder stuck in my jacket, close to my shoulder on the right arm. Whau! Now I began to have different thoughts about that puff adder. I realised that it had indeed accomplished its task, though it was still so inexperienced that its bite had not reached my flesh, but just brushed the hair; nonetheless, here was an exhibit of a large fang confirming that the puff adder had done all in its power to fight on behalf of its nation – it had lost its tooth for the sake of the nation of snakehood – and I so wished that I could see this puff adder again. I tried to think of my fellow men, grown men, young lads, our women and girls, and whether there was any one among them who had lost a tooth while fighting for their nation, but found none; I could not find even one who had lost a toe or a fingernail, not even one who had lost a hair for the sake of his people. I began to wonder what kind of nation we were that was being bettered, shown up by snakes when it comes to unity. The act of the puff adder was remarkable when you think that it did this work alone in the wilderness with nobody to encourage it, nobody to support, applaud or praise it for work well done. I then realised that at the time that it was hissing, it was not praising itself but was crying out to its ancestors to take care of it, in the injuries it had sustained that day for the sake of its nation, and I knew that its ancestors would forgive it.

3

In the afternoon

The dogs. – At this point, now already the afternoon of this summer day, I was still tossing around in my mind the events that I had experienced that morning. My body could already feel that I had had nothing to eat the whole day. Then I saw the house of a white man on the right side of the road and thought of turning in there to ask for something to eat, even if it was what he fed his dogs and pigs; I was hoping that perhaps I could buy something, no matter how much it cost, because I was in a severe state of hunger. While thinking about this, I moved towards the house, but, just a few steps into the turn-off, I saw that the two dogs of this white man had seen me; in my experience, two adult dogs were not usually that dangerous, but these two – I had invaded their space and their home – how was I going to handle them?

The white man's dogs came quietly, without barking, but I realised that they were not out to play. Meanwhile, inside the house, people jumped up and down, creating chaos, shouting at the dogs, trying to stop them; but it was as though these two dogs had closed their ears. Behind them, a few yards away, there was a man frantically calling after them, but what else could he do? Now these two lads came charging at me – while I stood stunned, not knowing what to do; there was no tree in sight, and it did not strike my mind that I should run back towards the gate. As they were running menacingly towards me, I prepared myself: rather have the consequences of my actions discussed later than allow myself to be ripped apart by dogs. Even the Bible says: "Save me from the claws of a dog." The moment they appeared in front of me, ready to lunge, I pulled out my umbrella instead of the knobkierie, and – see there! – in a split second, pressed it wide open, lifted it up and knelt down! And guess what? They fled, trampling each other's toes faster than when they had come charging at me, they ran back to the house, arriving one after the other! One was even limping because the man chasing them had aimed at it as they passed him and hit it on its side with a stone, and its leg had gone lame. This incident reminded me of a verse from the Bible which reads, "They will come to you with a common mission but will run away in seven different ways." Well, I quickly followed them, looking forward to meeting the people of this place, just in case these dogs decided to come back while I was still on my own. I was brave enough to go straight to the house of the white man because I noticed they had sympathy with me – even the man standing close to me was calling the dogs and throwing stones to prevent them from chasing me. Immediately after the dogs arrived at the house, though, I heard a gunshot, only to find that it was the owner of these dogs who had fired it; he left one of them dead as he was so angry about what they had done. When I arrived at the house, he was searching for the other dog while the first one was lying dead on the ground. I rushed to him, pleading for mercy, trying to speak his Boer language, asking him to forgive the second dog because they had not really hurt me. The Boer quickly went inside and asked me to follow. Once inside, I found the man in tears, praising the Lord for saving my life from these vicious dogs; while he was talking, he was holding my right hand and referring to me as his brother. Various dishes were prepared in the dining room by the daughter of this white man, and I was warmly invited to help myself to as much as I wanted. I certainly helped myself to the much I wanted, although my mind was confused – I was not used to this kind of gesture in a white man's house, nor being served by his daughter, so my mind was not really at ease about the situation. The children of this house appeared at different times with their mother, a lady who spoke isiXhosa fluently, and I slowly began to feel at ease because of their generosity, and I indulged in their conversations, enjoyed the meal, and learnt a lot until it was time to leave. They warmly released me, accompanied me halfway and showed me short cuts to the main road.

While I was travelling alone along the road, thoughts about the incidents that had occurred at the house all came to the surface. I remembered being told that the dogs were usually on a leash, but unfortunately on that day, their son Nicholas had accidentally let them loose without the knowledge of the older people. At the time of my arrival he was suffering his punishment.

I connected the actions of these dogs that had charged at me with the naive mentality of my fellow men, who, even when they had agreed on something, would later be distracted by an insignificant trifle, even though their mission was already known to the whole world. My people had not learnt to hold onto their mission resolutely, no matter the circumstances. Just look at these cowardly dogs leaving home with the intention of tearing me to pieces! They were reprimanded and rebuked but carried on charging at me, not heeding any warning as they focused on their important mission. And then? Then they were turned back by such a trivial thing as an umbrella, something that could not beat them, nor cut them, nor stab them; they were turned back by cowardice and stupidity.

With regard to the home of these dogs, it was the house of a Boer. Boers were known for their hatred of the black man and for despising him, but this home was the very place where a black visitor received hospitality without being charged. In addition to the Boers, other nations of the West believed this: "The life of a black man does not even compare with that of an ostrich or a white man's dog." But this Boer went to the extent of killing his dog for the sake of a black man, although it had not even bitten him. This act taught me that there is no nation that was created to be naturally cruel; there are good and bad people from all nations. Regarding the punishment of the dog by a stone and the shooting of the other one by his owner, indeed it was the punishment that cowards deserve for being distracted so easily.

What had made me so determined to go to that house? I somehow sensed that things were in my favour; indeed, it was just the way I felt. What does this mean? It means that a visitor is able to sense the atmosphere of a home: whether it favours him or not, even without a word being said. This phenomenon is known as the ability to assess the humanity of the home-owner. A person has no reason to feel proud of not being rude to a visitor. And the main concern should be the atmosphere in a home, not how plentiful the food is. Among Xhosa homes, there are some that are frequented by visitors, the reason for this being that visitors share their experience of their visits and encourage others by saying: "Should you get stranded, go to so-and-so's house for shelter because the doors are open, it is a home where you will find ubuntu." Remember that this does not refer to the food that one will receive, but rather the sense of human warmth, of ubuntu, of humaneness.

The boys. – As the sun was setting, my journey was close to its end as I was nearing my destination. In the field through which I was travelling, there was a group of cows grazing a piece of land; in front of me was a group of boys who were herding them. As I came closer, I noticed that there were two groups of boys: one group on this side of the road, and the other on that side. The older boys lined up sticks running from the one side of the road to where the other group was standing – and crossing these sticks was a kind of dare.

I approached them with a greeting, "Hello, young boys!" They responded from both sides, "Hello, Father!" I walked to the sticks lying in a line across the road, paused and asked why they were arranged like that. There were different answers: some said they didn't know, others said it was just for fun, and some said, "It's because of these other boys!" I saw others moving back and distancing themselves, suspecting that I was about to start a commotion by beating them up! I asked if the cows belonged to their homes. They said yes. I asked if they were studying. They said no. I asked why they were not studying, and again, there were different answers: some said their parents denied them the opportunity while others said they were not interested and would never go to school. I returned to the issue of lined-up sticks and asked them to each collect his stick. This practice of making a line with sticks was associated with big boys wanting to attack travellers; I warned them that they were still young and that they should refrain from this behaviour as they put their lives at risk and could be killed by travellers (although I could see that among them were grown-up boys). I returned to education because it concerned me that it was the very children of my nation who were not at school, while children of other nations were far ahead. I spoke tough words to them as if I was their father; I was so deeply moved that tears ran down my face. Then I chose to resume my journey and gradually vanished from their sight. Reaching some bushes, I knelt down and looked up to the Ntaba kaNdoda mountain; I don't remember all that I said, but I heard myself saying, "Accept my tears in your vessel of mercy," and I quickly stood up to walk towards the last river valley.

4
The girls

The girls. – As I came across the river valley, I met a group of girls perfecting the final touches of decorating themselves with traditional make-up[3] – and trying to outshine one another. Some were playing, others polishing their feet, others beautifying themselves, others having a conversation, while in the background a soothing song lingered softly. After having been so affected by my encounter with the boys, I now felt a rush of relief, enjoying the soul-catching sound, admiring the nimble feet which were being polished, the head-bands on the brushed hair, and the beautiful beadwork necklaces covering their chests. I had to admit that I could feel how my mood was changing when I crossed this valley.

Immediately when the girls saw me, they rushed together for a discussion while one of them shouted, "Come out, Tokazi, here is a young lad, we'll make him play our game!" I quickly took a look to one side and saw Tokazi joining the group, carrying a palm leaf, her mouth still stained black from the fruit that she had been eating. I could immediately feel that of all the girls who were blocking my way until I had chosen the one I fancied, I was attracted most to Tokazi. It was the time of year of which it is said, "A young man can't take one step without having to make a choice." But there I stood, absolutely stunned, staring helplessly at them as though I wanted to comply with their command. Oh! They all looked beautiful! I was not sure what occasion they were coming from but they looked striking, and in age they ranged from ten to twenty-one years. When they noticed that I was hesitating to follow their instruction, they harassed me, coming closer: "Cross over, young lad, make a choice and we will let you go!" Others were saying: "Choose the girl that will fetch water for you, or that will be your wife," while others suggested: "Choose the girl you love most among these!"

Others went so far as to suggest: "Choose a suitable wife for yourself!" I ended up saying in a soft voice: "My dear children, I have no knowledge of the things you are talking about, can you please make way for me?" I tried to push my way through as I was talking, but they had already formed a strong line of defence to prevent me from passing through, while at the same time painting my face with their cream, as if thinking that I was one of them. Eventually I agreed to obey their request but asked for an offering in return. They looked in their bags for some tobacco to offer, but I immediately grabbed the palm tree leaf from Tokazi. Goodness, the excitement they showed, clapping hands and rejoicing with Tokazi, all accompanied by great laughter and remarks: "He has chosen Tokazi!" "Oh, dear girl, you have won the game!" When the girls reached this point, I was actually delighted because, in truth, although I pretended to join the game simply because of their persistent requests, I was not really interested in participating in it, as I was preparing myself to talk about education as I had done with their brothers.

This Tokazi of the royal family, my brother, was ovally shaped, dark like a dagga pip, with long rich hair, long eyelashes and thick eyebrows and a small gap between the front teeth, about twelve years old. How beautiful were her well-formed teeth! She was not wearing any jewellery, no bangles, no necklaces, only woven grass around her neck which was not for adornment but had been made by her mother to cure a sore throat. At one stage Tokazi demanded her palm leaf back: "Give me my palm leaf!" and I said: "I will give it to you in due course, Tokazi!" In the background, the other girls burst into laughter: "Oh dear! They know each other already!"

At that moment, I changed the topic and asked who of them were still at school. They blushed and grinned, asking me the purpose of school, and ridiculed what they referred to as so-called Christians, but I kept reminding them that it was now my turn to talk because they had given me the platform. I explained how wonderful it would be to find them at school, especially because it was not far from their homes.

At home. – I left immediately while they were digesting my words, walked up through the bushes, walked fast without looking back – and again I made a detour to some bushes, knelt down, looking up at the Ntaba kaNdoda mountain, and said a few words on behalf of the young girls of my area. From there on I continued steadily until I arrived at my aunt's home just before the sun set.

My aunt's husband was the founder of the school in this village, together with the missionaries who were here before; he was therefore a highly respected man and was well known in this area and the neighbouring districts.

It so happened that by the following day – the day after my arrival – the whole village was aware of my visit. Although most people did not know me in person, they knew my father well from his frequent visits to my aunt, and as a result, many highly respected men and women and some young people visited me at my aunt's home, so it became known as a social place, where I was welcomed by the slaughtering of a goat. I began to share the events of my journey, what I had experienced, the good and the bad, but I related it in a very light-hearted manner.

On the third day of my visit, we heard that a family from the ochre people close to the school had brought their children to school, the parents claiming that they were forced by the desire of the children to go to school. This interest started with a few girls and boys, but grew quickly so that within the week that I spent at my aunt's home, there were already twenty boys who were attending school for the first time. This interest extended to the girls, who joined the school in growing numbers.

My heifer. – On the second day of my visit, while at the kraal with the head of the family and the eldest son, Thozamile, I was asked whether I still remembered the heifer, the young cow I was promised for my achievements at school about ten years before. "Of course I remember! Together, perhaps, with calves it might have had over the years?" The son interrupted, "The cattle you see there are the offspring of that cow ..." and he pointed at some cattle they were discussing. I was not yet this bearded man I am today, so I was amazed. There were fifteen head of cattle; apparently some had died recently, otherwise there would have been twenty. So for the rest of my stay, I was a herder, taking them to the veld and back.

Expansion of the school and the return home. – I was strongly reprimanded for my dangerous tendency to travel alone, especially to travel on foot. My aunt was extremely worried after hearing about the ups and downs of my journey and how I eventually arrived at her place. So when I returned to my own home, I travelled with a group of men who were on their way to the city to seek work. They helped me to escort my cattle, as I took them with me, leaving only one cow behind. This time it was really a pleasant journey, because to Xhosa people there is nothing more blessed for a man than to take time to visit relatives.

When I arrived home, it was as if I had been away to work in the city and had now returned for a holiday. Everybody was excited to see the wonderful gift I brought along, and the gesture of ubuntu that my aunt's husband had shown!

Over the years the good news continued: my aunt wrote in a letter that the school and church were demolished and a new, bigger school was built because the previous one became overcrowded, and the teachers had to be increased from one to five; I also learnt that the boys were grateful to the man whom they had challenged with the game of sticks. Apparently, about three of them are now teachers. As for the girls, I have learnt they were also pleased about the young man who played their game. As for Tokazi, there is not much to say; we live in the same house and she is now a minister in the Methodist Church; people, including me, call her Mfundisikazi, Minister, and she is fully qualified.

The villagers' homes, that used to be like those of the red ochre people, are now modern four-sided buildings, where you sit at a table for meals, sleep on comfortable beds, read newspapers, discuss current issues around government, agricultural and farming matters, and education as well as social issues from which one can get intellectual motivation and enjoyment. The news is that people of that village have a great desire for my return visit. According to them, this development is a result of my involvement.

In fact, I also want to go back to that place, but am still pre-occupied with certain challenges and demands. I will give you an update should I get a chance to go there. For now, *Goodbye, my friend.*

SECTION TWO

5

The journey begins

After some time, my challenges and commitments came to an end and I could return to the place I had once visited, my aunt's home within the Central Area, where the people were longing to see me – a feeling I shared. Here at home, the news of my visit was already the talk of the day, as if I was about to visit a sacred country. And, not surprisingly, when they heard about my forthcoming visit, everybody wanted to join me – indeed, if I had accepted every request, I would have left with the whole district, which would have put the host town in an impossible situation. On the other hand, it would have been a great pleasure for the people of the host town to meet a group of people from the rural areas, because people from the rural areas were respected in the towns. It was common practice for townspeople, Rhanuga people, who had grown up in rural areas to speak proudly of their home village; as a result, if one had just returned from a short visit home, one's friends would be curious to hear the news about everything back at home, and one would gladly share the developments.

After a few preparations, we took off, six of us, leaving behind my young wife and children. We boarded a train to the city that

I had visited previously on foot. Bear in mind that this time around, I was not visiting my aunt but was going to a different place, a place where one would have liked to be included as a member of the family.

The hospitality we received on our way showed that many people still led happy lives, despite the escalating taxes and the drought and diseases that were ruining many lives. We met different groups who came to greet us. Some brought provisions, others came with greeting cards, others with blessings from above which they read to us. All these things touched my heart, and I asked what I had done for them, to deserve these gestures. Truly, there was nothing I had done to deserve these compliments, because they were all self-sufficient, far wealthier than I; they had well-established homes, and some of them were well-respected elders with important credentials. I am saying this because it really touched me, but one also knew that a Xhosa child never forgot where he had received generosity; he would long to return kind gestures, even for generations to come.

6

At Zathuza city

We spent one day on the journey; by the afternoon of the next day, the train had arrived. As it approached the platform, we could see people who had come to meet us. The host had arranged a number of carts that would take us to where we would sleep for the night so that we could attend the special welcoming function organised for us with speeches and songs. There was also a greeting card with beautiful artwork that was read and given to us.

Part of the content of this card contained words and messages that surprised me. The speaker spoke of the "Patriot", a "Friend to the Nation", a "Leader." When the speech touched on these words, I became quite emotional and was filled with anxiety, shyness and embarrassment; I could not figure out how they had arrived at these inspirational names. In response to the speeches, I was lost for words – I felt so flustered and guilty that everything had been organised in honour of me, and was overwhelmed by such uncontrollable emotion that the handkerchief I was using was not enough – even a child could see that I was overcome.

I have already said that my response was insignificant, letting loose words with no direction, but all the same, this is what my words implied: "My dear friends, home of the chiefs, the words you have just said about me are beyond comprehension, I deserve none of them. I am not a hero because I have never fought for anything; nor have I been to war. I am not a leader, nor will I ever be one. My dear fellow men, it is futile to shower one another with praises and applause for no good reason, for by so doing we just destroy one another; we paralyse one another emotionally, because once a person hears such praises after he has done a certain task, he becomes big-headed, his mind pathetically deformed. And the actions of a mentally defective person are more useless than the crawling of a toddler. My dear fellow men, I so wish that I could be left as I am – to remain a loner and only join crowds on celebration days.

"I do not know what this gathering would have been like without the presence of the jocular fellows who accompanied me, fellows who, with their sense of humour, created a warm atmosphere everywhere we went; fellows who, in response to my words, polished my speech, raising it to a level of perfection, so that I now feel like standing up and shouting out loud, 'Oh yes, I said so, indeed!'"

The five gentlemen who came with me were men of integrity, and Christians; two of them were established farmers who owned farms; the third one was a highly talented man, but he did not own any land; another one was somebody familiar with city life, an ordinary man with no profession but who profitably used the knowledge he had acquired in the city. The fifth was an Evangelist at our church: he had accepted the word of God while growing up, was an expert in traditional legal proceedings, a popular figure in that field and also a traditional prophet. As for their stature: no one could complain about that!

We stayed awake the whole night at this gathering and dispersed in the morning to our different places, taking from the function what had been given to us: provisions for our long journey ahead. Again that night, there were hugs and hand-shakes all round as we took leave.

The time passed so quickly that the next day seemed to flash by; as was the tradition, visitors came in and out to feast on what was left. In the afternoon we were taken to see the tourist attractions of the city. Our intention to continue with the journey was completely ignored – to tell the truth, the hosts of the city we were heading towards were already here to fetch us, but were themselves so excited with the sightseeing that they didn't bother in the least with their actual task. From them we heard that the majority of the workers in this city were from that very city that we were heading for.

Readers will not believe how quickly, in the two days that we had so far spent in Zathuza city, we felt that we also belonged here in this community and had come to know all the issues affecting workers. The next thing we did was to write and publish an article in the main daily community newspaper, highlighting unfair labour practices by company owners, involving black workers; we suggested what good labour relations should really look like to benefit both workers and employers. And things didn't stop there. The next minute, it was the establishment of a men's society, the Manyano, or the Union of Young Men, for financial investments, and one for girls on domestic education; then it was time for the great Revival[4] and Fasting campaign.

And indeed, very soon after, we received a letter from the city's mayor who humbly invited us to a council meeting regarding the article published in the newspaper. Apparently the council was impressed and felt that a joint meeting would provide an opportunity to discuss these suggestions in detail.

Off we went to this meeting, a delegation of seven men: three of us visitors, and the remaining four our hosts. What was coming our way seemed a miracle. On meeting the council, I was relieved: it was as though we had known each other for a long time, and they approved all the recommendations in the article written by this man-from-Xhosaland. The council allocated a large empty site to us in order to build a structure for the nation-building organisation that we had established for the youth; the building was to become a home for those who came to look for work, an information office for the chiefs, and recruitment offices for employment services; the officials here were to be black men and women. The plot was located close to the black people's residential area, not far from town, because agricultural activities would be used to teach people of this area. However, what intrigued me most was that the allocated plot was at exactly the place where I had my first confrontation with the police so many years ago. And indeed, I tracked down that same black policeman who had harassed me, to take care of agricultural equipment for a good salary.

At this time, the Revival and Fasting Movement made a great impact on the lives of those citizens, and many souls were saved. The campaign went on for seven days, and it was so hectic that it seemed as if a whirlwind was moving things around, turning things upside down, and so the seven days felt to me like seven years.

Certain taxes were reduced, black people were reimbursed with large sums of money by the city council, and many good job opportunities for men and women were created, and these were all permanent jobs.

7

In the robbers' forest at Mgudu

When we eventually managed to leave, it was with crowds of people who wanted to accompany us: some on foot, others on horseback and some with their horse-drawn carts, some using their own horses and others hiring them. The city council also made a contribution to this journey and donated two big carts with drivers and horses for an unlimited period. Again, I became quite emotional when I saw the large crowd following us, because it was easy, out of excitement for an event, to take a day off from work, only to find yourself dismissed when you returned. I raised these concerns but my advice fell on deaf ears; instead people did what they wanted and continued with the journey.

The place where I had encountered the police earlier on was in the Zimba valley, so I was gratified to see that a big educational centre for our people had been established there, which was instrumental in creating job opportunities for the unemployed. The building project was already in progress and some houses had been sold.

When the large crowd took to the road, it was as if they were following a statesman. We continued in this way until we reached the area of the thick forest where I was once nearly attacked by robbers, and the gorge known as Mgudu. But this time around, whenever I tried to locate this forest, I kept seeing new houses built in the modern way; when I looked to the other side, I saw an avenue with trees lined up on both sides of the road; down the valley a massive agricultural project had been established. It all looked breathtaking and fresh, different from the place I had known. It was an educational institution on a site bought by the church to build its own school; a church had also been erected there. Behind these buildings was a house for student accommodation and where cotton production, weaving and knitting were taught. Trees used especially for making woven chairs and baskets were cultivated in the valley as well as different types of grass for specific uses by the community. The cleaning of sheepskins and goatskins was done here, and shoes were made, as well as woven and knitted shawls and blankets. These products were produced through hard labour, because there was no equipment; everything was handcrafted or made on small machines.

Even before we arrived there, we were told to stay for at least a day. Just as we crossed the river with its sweet waters below the houses, we encountered a mass of students in two long queues, stretching for half a mile to the houses in a guard of honour on both sides of the road. While we were waiting outside, a welcome speech was read to us, highlighting contributions we had made to the town that we had just left, and encouraging us to continue our good work.

In reply, we congratulated the community for the important things they had done and said it would be a great pleasure to learn more about them. After we had refreshed ourselves, we went to the tearoom and from there were taken to see dams, plants, agricultural production, and buildings, and were shown an account of their costs, annual income and expenditure. Once we had heard everything, we realised that these gentlemen carried a great financial burden and could hardly support their own families or buy themselves clothes. When we arrived that day, the project was on the verge of closing down because it did not get any external assistance – the government refused to give support, although it did once send an official to assess the administration and the conditions, and possible support was promised, but that was the end of it.

We were told that it was difficult to sustain the place financially, and that things had become worse after the death of the key figure – he had maintained everything, even using some of his own money. After his death his possessions were distributed among his family members; this was a mere token, as he was not a wealthy person. We heard that 200 black families lived here; however, this number could have multiplied five times if the conditions had been conducive. But now it was impossible to add even one room for accommodation or for a class.

We had a special welcome gathering on that first night. Oh yes, there were good and bad things! We learnt that the two chief officials here had been among those boys who had laid out sticks on the road where Don Jadu, the traveller, once passed. After the interesting gathering we were left to reflect on the conditions of this place.

The first thing the man-from-Xhosaland wanted to know was whether the church would be willing to hand over the place to be used by the community and the many other religious denominations. They acknowledged that, on behalf of the whole community, the idea had already been approved, provided it did not retard developments. The community was asked what kind of assistance they wanted. But they had not yet arrived at any decision, because other communities had become involved and also needed to be consulted. They wanted to know their options, and said that in general they wanted things to remain as they were: work conditions were fine, but there was one thing problem, and that was the decline in the value of their products. They said they would appreciate it if none of the workers were laid off, and that additional workers, stronger and more powerful, should be appointed, and some more training courses added.

Eventually a conclusion was reached, after the history of the church and the story of its establishment about ten years earlier had been explored. By dawn the following morning, the following resolutions were arrived at:

1. This homestead would no longer be a school for only one particular church.
2. As from this day, the homestead would be interdenominational.
3. The Manyano, the Union of Young Men, in the process of being established in town, should be a branch of this interdenominational homestead.
4. There would be no changes in the policy of this homestead, except those relating to expansion.
5. There should be an in-house doctor and a hospital.
6. A nursing college should be added as soon as possible.
7. A letter of recommendation should be sent to the government requesting its assistance in the establishment of the above.

We left there with this good news and promised to use our influence to ensure that the men in authority should receive their salaries immediately, backdated to the previous months, since they had already had six months without payment. By the time we left, it was as though they had been visited by angels, so they said.

We left with applause, shouts of excitement and the music of the brigade's band until we gradually disappeared from the scene, leaving behind people ululating "Huntshu!" As for me, a man so sceptical about things, I forced myself to come to my senses: these were men of calibre, which was why they were so excited. Having said these words, I very much wished to be alone so that I could express my emotions – so that I could cry out loud and pray. But there was no opportunity.

8

At the Boer's homestead at Zuba

We were heading home with no expectation of any interruption along the way. Our bodies were looking forward to relaxing – especially my body, the body of a rural person not familiar with the glitter and the bustling noises of the city – but to my surprise to this day, we did not reach home.

In the middle of nowhere, at a place called Siganga, there where I had seen ostriches fighting over domestic matters and where they had seen me; where I had challenged the wire fence, introduced myself to the puff adder and received insults from the Boers, there was still a gate linking two sites. When we entered the gate I heard somebody saying, "Loosen the horses!"

Indeed, loosening took place, although I could not see any reason for that. The Boers with me rejoiced at seeing this place, and I kept pointing out the gorges that I had once passed through in my escape from the ostriches, and where I had soared to unknown heights after being attacked by the puff adder. The place was just as it was before, nothing had changed with time; the shrubs on which I had sprawled were still there, and ostriches were still feeding there, but today we feared them not. I could even say that they were the ones who feared us, as we were quite an army.

Just when we were about to leave, the deep voice of the men was heard saying that it would be very convenient if a hotel could be established here, an expensive one, and also that there should be shops and other developments. When I asked who would sponsor this in this desolate area, a well-prepared answer came up: if the two sites here were to be taken, erven could be marked off for building and divided into plots for a residential area. As they spoke, they pointed at the land surveyor who could subdivide the sites. Even the manager of this future hotel was known – he was among us – and they wanted this project to be run by the Organisation of the Youth in town.

We continued as a large crowd. Although some went back to their jobs in town, it did not make any difference, because the numbers who joined were greater than those who turned back. Late in the day, I noticed that the group in front was turning right, exactly at the entrance that I had turned into when I was met by the Boer's two sweating male dogs.

But now I realised that some development had also taken place at that Boer's homestead: the gate that joins the road was something to see, and there was a row of trees on both sides leading up to the homestead, and, yes, had they been there many years earlier, things would have been different. I could not resist the thought that if only these trees had been planted long ago, I could have climbed one of them to escape the dogs and saved myself some trouble. We reached a very big homestead with renovated houses, not the ones I knew. When we stopped, people were moving around busily there, like a flock of birds, and you could see that the people were local. What was most significant was the multitude of palm trees; they were planted beautifully and enclosed the homestead like a woven mat of palms.

What was this homestead for? The reader will ask that, and people in our group also asked: "Now what is this establishment?" "What is it for?"

This farm had been bought from the children of the kind Boer by a black man who happened to be Tokazi's elder brother; he was determined to revive and beautify it, and build a new house, but also that the farm should not be limited to beauty only: projects should be carried out on it.

So apparently the first thing this man did was to plant trees, as we could see, and he established forests. After that he designed bricks and taught others how brick-making was done; people also came from afar to learn how bricks were made, how stone carving was done and how to build with brick and stone. Another thing that was practised was to scald animal skins, scrape them and then make shoes, using the old Boer method of making hide shoes.

The group there were hard-working people who had once worked for the Boers, and they knew about beautiful things and were trying to make them. Some wore skin blankets that stretched from the feet up to the neck, and it became obvious that this group was somewhat vain, admiring all new things. Most of them made these blankets themselves. A person would soften the hide until it became like blanket cloth. They also made their own shoes, and hats of animal skin; the women made elegant blue duiker head coverings that high-class women of the olden days wore. We loved the things we saw at this place, and they became a sign of new things to us; we fervently wanted progress to be made with these things, in keeping with present times.

When we arrived at this homestead, the horses were untied and stabled and fed; we were walked to our rooms, which were distributed among the houses, and we all fitted in despite being so many. At about sunset, after we had rested in this calm atmosphere and refreshed ourselves, horses from the farm were harnessed and we were driven around the establishment to see everything: dams, fountains, fields, plantations, orchards, and many other things.

We were shown a place where bricks were made, by being mixed with grass to make them solid; we were shown places where stones of certain beautiful types were being mined to build expensive houses. We were satisfied by the things we saw here, although we could not determine their standard. The implements for ploughing and planting needed to be replaced by new ones, as the soil was terrible and stony, and needed to be worked extensively. Most of the buildings were in the old style of the Boers, and most of the people spoke Afrikaans, and the issue of schooling was far beyond their thoughts. Although there were some faults, we praised the things we saw; also, when we considered that they were just the small efforts of black people who were not highly educated and who were not assisted by anyone, we felt their successes were enough to ensure they would progress.

When we were alone, we felt that what had been discussed at previous establishments should be tried here, that is, to buy this farm from the man of the Tshawe clan, and turn it into another establishment of the Organisation of the Youth that was based in town. Because we had already added establishments to our project, we mistakenly thought that we could do more than we actually could, though the organisation had not yet expanded through its own work.

That night, instead of having a gathering with songs and plays, we were involved in discussion about the issues we were still considering, namely how to advance this establishment. To our surprise, the local men came in droves, and we could see that they were in very good health and keen.

We did not talk a lot. We tried to show that development is something that should begin at home: it starts there. Therefore each man had to sacrifice what he had, the very thing that he perhaps loved most, so that when the thinking about development took place, it already had a foundation. The men from Zuba heard us, and they did not hear us negatively.

Before the night was far advanced, things had become easy, especially as there was an urge to help right from the beginning:

a man sacrificed his two *astros* (*agterosse*, oxen that were harnessed at the back of the team). The next one sacrificed his two *foros* (*voorosse*, oxen harnessed at the front of the team); then the next one abandoned his wagon and its two horses; the next one took his money bag and took out fifty pounds (£50). These men gave and gave, calmly rivalling each other; we were amazed and deeply touched, as they were contributing devotedly, and – indeed! the money already amounted to 2 000 pounds (£2 000)! As we were about to finish that night, the total amount had reached 3 100 pounds (£3 100). It was also indicated that there were still other men who were absent, but who would be informed, and there was much hope that they would contribute. We then went to our sleeping places so that we would be ready to wake up in the morning and go to the meeting.

During the late morning, at about ten o'clock, the meeting resumed and accepted the following decisions:

1. The Organisation of the Youth, whose headquarters were in the town, in Zathuza, was buying this farm, so that it became its subsidiary.
2. Of the profit accumulated through this project, each man who had contributed something had to receive something back, with interest, if that was approved.
3. Workers and managers of this project had to be from this area, except experts who could be recruited from elsewhere.
4. The aim would be to advance the small projects that had already been executed, and to add some as the project expanded.

When this wonderful short meeting closed, we wanted to gather our belongings as we were still far from where we were going. By the time we had finished lunch, our belongings were packed. The owner of this farm told us that he had already negotiated with the owners of the farms at Siganga, and that they would meet with him at a dilapidated house in the place where the puff adder and the ostriches had been, the place earmarked for the hotel. He said that they would decide on written transactions, both for selling and buying. The group encouraged him strongly, telling him not to delay, and that no opportunity for education in that beautiful district should be missed.

9

At Mnandi

The team was now bigger and busier than it had been, as the time of our arrival at Mnandi had been announced. It was clear that the day's weather would not be fine; we could expect thunder and hail. People from Mnandi were already here to meet us, riding on carts and horses. And the team from the Royal House also came, as big as an army, and said that there had been excitement in the city since we had left. The team from Zuba also came in droves, leaving behind whatever had happened on the way to Mnandi. We immediately appreciated that Mnandi was a place that was important to everybody in those districts; whenever you met anyone, you heard him claiming that Mnandi was his home, and others confirmed it.

When the sun was over the mountain, we approached the homestead, and saw that it was not so far away – the distance was about a mile or less. But – watch out! The weather was not going to allow us to arrive safely. All of a sudden there was a tornado, a great whirlwind, causing havoc in every direction; it churned up dust, and the sky became so dark that it was twilight before twilight's time. It was impossible to go further! In the panic, carts, horses and people became entangled and – remember – there were a lot of people: a procession of schoolchildren lining up for us, another group that was to sing with their teachers, yet another set running up and down preparing for our arrival; but now even horses blundered into one another, trying to escape the turmoil. It was clear that things were becoming dangerous.

The reader will understand that we were about to reach Mnandi. But how? How did we arrive? These questions became unanswerable. What happened was extraordinary. Where did you arrive? At what did you arrive? Houses? Never! Those questions were impossible to answer, because actually, we arrived nowhere, we found ourselves all over and dispersed, not even recognising one another – side-stepping a bolting horse, escaping things that had collapsed and were being whirled about by the wind, trying not to crash into each other.

At the Mnandi homestead, various decorated platforms were waiting for us; from a distance, we saw them collapsing, and their parts being scattered away. Platforms created for speakers and their supporters and for musicians were all blown away by the wind and became treacherous menaces. In that chaos one could hear the voices of women frantically calling their children. Pieces of half-built houses and roof sheets of corrugated iron became dangerous weapons bouncing sharply around.

The reader will appreciate that pots of food were already lined up outside for our arrival. As the terrified horses were dashing up and down with nobody directing them, carts crashed and shattered into pieces, never to be reassembled! People and pots of food and horses were colliding and clashing! We immediately asked people to sit down where they were at that moment and then asked some young men to accompany them to safer houses. That took a lot of time.

The cattle were not far from the homesteads as they were returning from the veld. What did they do? That was something else to fear, because they stormed savagely, running as if they were berserk! They were wild and bellowing crazily. Others got caught in the horses' ropes. That created more havoc – cattle and horses and ropes!

My friend who reads this book will understand that the people caught up in this mayhem were strangers to each other; they had never seen each other. Before the storm they were dressed in fine apparel; but would you say that now? Not at all! They were filthy and you would not know them, dirty, dusty, and some were bleeding, but even for bleeding there was no time – it was cuts on the head caused by knocks and blows, it was blows on the head caused by hitting against things, it was wounds, it was shouting and panting! Everybody was saying: "It's Judgement Day today!"

At that moment, suddenly, the biggest danger erupted, though not unexpectedly. There were abrupt, loud cries. What was that now? Fire! During this havoc the fires had been forgotten! Burning pieces of firewood were whipped around by the wind and sparks spattered. The wood packed for later use caught fire and simply swallowed everything lying around. The fire also reached the kraals. E-e! When the terror hit people, the fire had already spread and become a major peril. What was all this?

Some, when they took fright, took things from their houses and threw them outside. When others became afraid, they took things that were outside and threw them inside their houses; according to *their* judgement the fire was outside! Indeed, there was a lake of fire within the homestead! The wind gave no indication of subsiding, and the night was coming. People were taking things and putting things down without any purpose. There was pulling and shoving. It was relentless, and became ever more relentless! All of us were fighting the enemy of the whole tribe: fire. Men's beautiful moustaches and their long thick whiskers were scorched. Eyelashes and eyebrows were burnt and left a smoothness where they once were. Legs and hands swelled, and things were in total confusion. Despite the hysterical panic, people tried to fix things; they were busy working, and they battled.

In the midst of that tumult a man's voice was heard: "Where are all these people coming from?" Another one said in a soft, frightened voice: "My Lord, we are all going to get killed!" At this point the young men were divided into two teams: one group went to the river to fetch water. The other was making mud, throwing that and wet bags and cloths on the flames. This broke the strength of the fire, and a short while after sunset the fire was defeated, and the wind finally subsided.

Then the teams began to restore the situation by taking, where possible, scattered things back to their places. They also did their best to prepare places for the visitors to rest, because they were sympathetic towards us for being caught up in this chaos; the visitors, too, were sympathetic towards those working so tirelessly because of them.

Pronouncements and declarations followed, one after the other. Each person expressed his opinion; each expressed his thoughts. Some were saying that this occurrence was an omen, a prediction of a coming peril! Some were saying that this was a man-made misfortune, a spell destroying good deeds; whoever did it wanted houses to fall on people so that they could burn and die together. Others were saying it was an evil spell destroying good things because people praised one another instead of praising the evil powers. Satan was only satisfied when people fought and bit one another like dogs – so he brought down his wrath in the same way that he caused the houses to collapse on the sons and daughters of Job!

There were many opinions and speeches made by people about this. The main belief was: "Today is Judgement Day." We, too, had our opinions with regard to this matter. We said, "No, we have received a very great welcome from this country, something that caused the foundations of this place to tremble!"

As we were scrambling around, some people fled to sleep on the stony hillsides and in the forests; they, too, did not know one another there; they, too, were scrambling around just like us. Some of them said: "It must be a war!" Seeing the horses scattered all over, it looked to them as though an army was chasing them. They abandoned their homes. As the landscape burned, they assumed it was the enemy burning their homes, so in fear they crossed big rivers. Indeed, some were seen only after seven days, coming from where even they themselves did not know.

And then there were those chased away by the myth of all myths! In our group coming from Xhosaland there were two men from the Zima clan. While they were on their way, some people were jokingly saying: "It's an army of the Zima clan." And then somebody mentioned that, by the way, the Zimas[5] were cannibals. So people began insisting: "Where are those men-eaters you are talking about?" It turned out that these tales prejudiced people with simple minds, because, yes, they had heard in their grandmothers' fables that people of the Zima clan were indeed human-eaters. When the procession from Xhosaland approached, a person said: "The cannibals are coming!" Initially it was not an issue; but when the visiting group approached with such force and mayhem, some people thought that what they had heard from their grandmothers was finally fulfilled – that was how one's home was destroyed! So each one fled in haste, running away with nothing, protecting only his own soul.

When the wind toppled big trees in the veld, those simple-minded people understood the truth: here was the dust that was always spoken of, indicating the coming of the cannibals. Here were the fires and the smoke – therefore be not sceptical about cannibalism, we are surrounded by human-eaters. So in the veld, groups attacked one another because they did not know one another; they had not left together, and they were scaring each other. Those who were running away from the war were scared of those who were running from the Zima clan. Those who fled from the Zima clan were scared of those who had fled from the war.

Among the people who ran away from the human-eaters was Zakade's father – a man with one eye; the other had been wounded by gunshot when he was still young. And don't even talk about his anger! When he returned after ten days, he wanted to stab people when they talked about his escape. But he was the one who initially narrated his story of fleeing to different forests and steep, stony hillsides. When he arrived at his sister's place at Ceme, across the Zitshangane, the people there pacified him.

10

After the storm

After the tornado and the storm, after the crash of carts and small wagons, and the breaking of ropes; yes, after people were injured falling from their horses; after the fires and burning of people's bodies, houses and kraals, it was quiet; there was complete silence. By then it was already deep dusk. People, that is visitors and locals, were so exhausted that they had to go to their resting places. Great gratitude was shown to the Almighty, Ndikhoyo, because, despite all that had happened, no soul was lost.

There was, indeed, very little harm done, considering how fierce things had been: precisely four horses died, five were seriously injured and nothing could be done to help them; the three calves tied to the kraal died without anybody noticing. Gxasheka of the Bhele clan fell into the lake while hurrying to get water to extinguish the fire. It turned out that he could not swim, and the coat he was wearing was very heavy and it pulled him down to the bottom; the group only noticed what was happening to Gxasheka when he was about to drown, and they quickly pulled him out and laid him on his stomach, turning him upside down. That helped immediately: the water gushed out through his mouth, but he did not recover immediately.

Bhozi from the Thunzini clan was hit on his shoulder by a burning beam which lay across his body and crushed him beneath, but eventually that was also noticed and water was poured on him, cooling him off. Hletyiwe from the Vundle clan, an elderly woman, was found running up the hill in flames, her dress burning. When the fire was extinguished, she was carried down with some parts of her left side badly burnt. Ponoyi from the Ntakwenda clan heard a calf bellowing from the roof of a house; when he dived into the fire, untying the rope around the calf, the roof caved in and obstructed the doorway; he rushed through the flames at the back of the house while the calf jumped through another ball of flames and ran, but it collapsed and died. Ponoyi escaped without a single burn, with only a few bruises.

Sanityi's father, Oom Dirk (a coloured person), who was intoxicated from what he had consumed, slept by the fireplace and only woke up when the galloping horses jounced and crashed the pots – but he didn't wake up properly – just picked up meat that was there and ate, and did not bother about what was happening; he was just eating and talking to himself, not concerned at all. Anyone who came closer would have heard him mutter, "Ar mar, mna, ek es rona kaffir, ek es mense." But that destitute man sobered up after being seriously crushed by a horse trampling his chest. Imagine a man with a mouthful of meat, and holding more in his hands, waking up that night vomiting blood, feeling a huge bump on his forehead, and having no idea how it came about – that was the type of misfortune that occurred, and which we deemed not as serious as what could have happened, given the havoc, and we were very grateful to the Almighty, Ndikhoyo.

Indeed, when we went to bed that night all was quiet and calm, but it turned out that local men and women did not sleep at all: right through the night they were fixing the storm damage. They worked all night so that by morning all would be restored, and indeed when we, the visitors, woke up, the place was beautifully decorated just as it had been before the storm, with the platforms set up. The trees seemed fixed in the ground as if they had grown overnight, and even the backdrop looked beautiful, the day being bright and ideal for the event. All the wreckage and dead horses had been collected and disposed of. Both of the carts from town were crushed beyond repair, and one horse from town had broken his front leg and had been shot the night before, but the others were well and in good shape. When this matter was later reported in town, the town council released everything to us, the surviving horses, bridles, and the remnants of the carts, saying the visitors' impact on their community was far greater than the value of those carts and horses.

After breakfast, just as the sun started to warm the place up, people were moving around at the meeting place. Carts and horses crossed the market place where the victims were still receiving help. There were groups from different places who had experienced the storm while travelling, but had fortunately found places to stay overnight, continuing their journey in the morning. Many processions of young men and boys passed by, marching in step and arranged in well-ordered lines, blowing trumpets and beating drums, every single one dressed in uniform. As soon as everyone had gathered, there was silence and we were fetched. We walked under trees that had been erected overnight, with long banners of cloth adorning the place, and hanging decorations. The homestead was filled with written notices which I recall meant, "Bring my palm tree leaf" and "Tokazi's palm leaf!" and "Tokazi and her palm tree branch", persistent reminders to me of the playful bargain Tokazi and I had struck at the river. There was also a big placard in the middle of this place saying: "You will get back your palm leaf, Tokazi, next time!" When this placard was hoisted it was placed in the middle, and drums were beaten, trumpets were blown, and people agreed that coming to this event was a good decision. Eventually when we sat down, it became quiet.

Written speeches from different organisations were read to us. They spoke of events from twenty years earlier, when this was still a desolate place with people who had no leadership, and who were uninformed and in the dark although they thought they were enlightened – until a fearless man sent by the Creator-of-all-things came to our area. When the boys lined up sticks for him, he did not flee or isolate himself, but simply stepped forward and began to teach, standing on them.

When the brave man left, he carried all the darkness of his people, and raised it up to heaven as a burnt offering, there by *that* bush – which was pointed out. And so we discovered that we were close to that very same bush; that bush, in the meantime, had been regarded by the people there as a holy place because a certain man had fallen on his knees there and prayed for God's intervention, and God had, indeed, intervened. A local man gave full details of this and explored the developments even further; then the remaining part of the story was completed by people of another group. They also mentioned a brave man who, when told of the mischief of darkness by local girls, had brought out light.

When the people talked about our activities in the town of Zathuza, they gave clear details, and then they came to the conclusion that there was a desire for even more development here than at Zathuza.

So when they gave me an opportunity to respond, I suddenly froze completely, confused; as if up to now I had not heard any of the speeches that had been made. Meanwhile people waited, eyes wide open, ears sharpened, waiting to hear a word from me – this man about whom they'd heard great things – and some had travelled long distances to see him with their own eyes. Noticing my loss for words, one of our loquacious brothers got up and joked about a bit, mentioning some of the highlights of our journey, and in general, brightening the mood.

He had hardly sat down when up sprang another brother who insisted that the man everyone had come to honour was destined for greatness; but this man had kept the story to himself and did not share it with anybody at home. The history narrated here, he said, was unknown to us in Xhosaland; all the things revealed today, this man had done alone, and hearing this was news to the audience. He spoke on this topic until I recovered fully.

As soon as he had sat down, I stood up, and spoke of my first visit twenty years earlier, which even then had not been my first here; but that visit had included rather unusual events. I spoke of my way of life back at home and commented on a few insignificant incidents happening in Xhosaland. I referred to some of the events that had occurred since I was last here, and at this point noticed that there were people in the audience so intently following me that when I pointed, they pointed; when I looked down, they looked down. I felt the people were with me and I felt strengthened.

Now I spoke about the journey from home to here, my objective for coming, and the wish of the gentlemen with me to see their fellow countrymen who seemed as if they were from a foreign country. I did not miss the opportunity to introduce them, saying who they were and what their professions were. Then the details of entering the city of Zathuza were given, what we did there and the reasons behind it; I touched upon our blessing in Mgudu and at Zuba, and also mentioned the documents from the government promising help. My last words were, "The spirit of our ancestors has followed us throughout this expedition, and our greatest wish is that it does not abandon us now that we have arrived in Mnandi."

After sitting down, I felt a sigh of relief from everyone. Today I felt that what I had said went to the soul, and I rejoiced. For the first time I felt emancipated and not overwhelmed by a sobbing heart; right up to the end I had everyone eating from the palm of my hand, each one of them following attentively. As I sat down I felt relieved of the pressure I had been under.

But now in the audience, some members were dangling in anticipation. They jumped up and down and fell, hitting the backs of their heads; there were those who hailed and whistled, not really knowing what for. Some stood up for no reason, in awe, pointed in my direction, then pointed at nothing in particular. There was a big crowd making a distant noise, again insistently directed at me: "Remember Tokazi with her palm leaf!" Everyone in the meeting joined the chant: "Tokazi with her palm leaf! Her palm leaf! Her palm leaf!"

On that day none of my fellow countrymen had to stand up as usual to clarify my words; even when I looked around, no, I found them with their heads hung low, looking down. I could see my words had had an effect; they felt moved and deep in thoughts I did not know. A minute of silence passed, nothing was said or done – until I stood up again and made a few witty and humorous remarks to put everyone at ease and release them, because clearly I had made everybody anxious.

Then a few began to mumble, although nothing much was said. Suddenly at that moment, drums played and we saw young men gracefully stepping in unison, performing supple, amazing movements. We couldn't imagine when they had been taught to do this; these men had already completed their schooling and we know that even in government schools movements like this were not taught.

After a while we dispersed to our respective rooms and were promised to be shown around that afternoon, and be entertained with songs, education and plays in the evening. The next day we were to be taken to the beach about ten miles from Mnandi.

As the sun set that day, the horse-drawn carts were readied and we toured the grazing lands and their borders, structures built by the people, such as dams – something needed in countries where, during a drought, there are no rivers with water. We were shown streams of water, man-made forests, nature reserves that were kept pristine so that even in winter most of the trees were green. We were shown sown fields and grain pits for storing food; in truth, we found that last year's maize was no different from that of this year; nor was the sorghum. Beans also had grain pits to preserve them, and these grain pits were different from the ones we know in Xhosaland. We moved around seeing where they had planted wild mint, African mahogany – the tamboti tree –, crane flowers, wild thyme, igusawe, itsawe, and other small plants that are familiar herbs. We were shown schools, churches, kraals for certain kinds of livestock, especially cattle and horses, and lastly the fields where physical exercises were done.

That evening there were masses of people who came to the song gathering; when there was no space anymore, some accepted that they had to be outside, and they were the same in number as those inside; beautiful songs were sung, and we were astonished by this place that one knew was so far from educational and developmental centres. The dance performances amazed us the most. Speeches were made by the owners of the homestead to welcome us and wish us a successful journey back to our homes; we also responded with good wishes. As the evening came to a conclusion, people dispersed, with the decision that the next day would be spent at the beach.

11

Work begins

Early the following morning, people were busy with a sense of urgency, as if they were migrating, preparing for the day on the beach. Some left at dawn in order to prepare a suitable place there for gathering and resting. The team of inspanned oxen also left early that morning, followed by the horses and horse-drawn wagons; the carts left after breakfast – and that long, straight line moved slowly, sometimes stopping, and for those watching, this became tiring, so they set off again and travelled until they reached the sea.

Here they settled and then walked around the beach, exploring, in particular, the Mnandi harbour. It was a joyful day with a lot of gatherings and discussions – and men rescued people from the water like bees pulling nectar from flowers. A big announcement was made of a meeting to take place the following day. People returned to Mnandi, but in larger numbers, as some additional visitors from all around the area had invited themselves to the hosting household. There was nothing to do during that evening, so that everyone could have a rest and prepare something well thought-through for the conference the next day.

To have a rest! Yes, I too welcomed the word "rest" as did the others; but actual rest was as rare as the tooth of a chicken. My aunt's sons were here; their sisters were married here, and their daughters as well; that made a network of my nieces and nephews, and *their* nephews and nieces, whom I had to see to discuss our own family matters. It was obvious to others that the Rhanuga situation in which people work for long periods on the Boer farms was difficult, and they were asking about a place to go to in Xhosaland. My advice was that they should seek a place in an area that they knew and were familiar with; to start making a living in a totally new place in these trying times is something one might regret and rebuke oneself for later. There were those who wanted me to adopt their children so that I might raise them in the ways of living in Xhosaland. That seemed to be my designated task, and I welcomed those children with open arms.

Some asked what had happened to the large number of cattle that I had received as a reward when I left. Had they not died because of people's incompetence in my area? My answer was straight: "I've never seen cattle multiplying like those cattle, they are big news to all the men in that whole area. They did not die; what they did was to give birth repeatedly, and their calves survived and gave birth too. The bull lived for years, and, as if it had received special traditional protective medicine, it behaved amazingly: unusually and unnaturally, it refused to mate with cows from other households. In brief, I can say that those cattle multiplied and multiplied until there were too many, so I had to rent extra veld for grazing. Yes, my aunt's cattle continued to amaze me, producing such a large number of offspring that I could send some to the butchery. With the two spans of oxen with their bullock-carts that I sold, I bought the two farms I own now – and those two farms are full of cattle. I hope these cattle will make a real person of me. It's obvious that I was given them with a pure heart. I was told that the heifer that I left behind had also kept multiplying, as had her offspring. Good heavens, was it not these heifers that enabled me to provide for the traditional ceremony with Tokazi's Tshawe clan?

There were many others also with questions; some wanted to know why I looked so young, because they had heard about me and my activities for such a long time. Well, I was exposed to politics at a young age, and, by being alert and diligent, adapted to advance intellectually and in knowledge. Some wanted to know what had led to my surprise visit here. I said I had been visiting my aunt and that it was not the first time. "Were you not afraid of the boys who made a line of sticks for you because they were of your age group?" "Yes, I can tell you; I was intimidated, but to me it was clear that I shouldn't retreat simply for personal survival, and I didn't."

"Did you take note of Tokazi on that day?" "A lot, when my eyes looked at her, there was no error nor fault, anyway I loved the fact that she was a true Xhosa maiden like any other Xhosa maiden." "When did you observe her so attentively?" some asked jestingly. "Actually, in places of education in Xhosaland; I saw her there a second time and initially did not recognise her because she had grown and changed – but I was crazy about her and heard later that she was that Tokazi from Msibeni. Since I already had a head painfully filled with love, it was obvious that I could finally get the right remedy."

"Is that what you are saying now, my man?" asked a man from the Rhanuga people.

"What am I saying? It depends on what *you* and your family here are saying; you are the narrators and doers of it!"

"What about the state of disunity that we from the Great Place are experiencing? Even from those who live here, I've never heard that visitors have come to negotiate lobola or to request permission here, as you did at the Great Place, to marry one of the chief's daughters."

"That, sir, also confused me, because when we recently talked about 'requesting a girl for marriage' we got an answer that surprised us: 'The whole ritual has been handed to the missionaries where the young woman resides,' and we said, 'But this was the Rhanuga people's way of doing things.' Nevertheless, we were quite satisfied with the missionaries; they executed the ritual well, to its conclusion."

"In your case, don't you think the attraction for them, the missionaries, was the wealth of the homestead of the Great Place?"

"I didn't see signs of that, sir, knowing them and their people – they have not stopped visiting us, and our men were always present with the missionaries when we were lawfully interrogating this matter. The story was that the missionaries did not want this woman to move and go home because of her usefulness to them."

"In which school was this young woman?" one asked. Another man from the Rhanuga people said cheerfully: "At St Matthews[6], of course!"

I have said that "resting" was just a word; because on this day, our task was to set up a hard-working team whose size was, as yet, unknown. It seemed that this place had a large number of youths who could be recruited, and this was something we did wherever we went; this was also typical of the other places we visited.

Then some neighbouring white farmers arrived, saying that they had heard that there were some chiefs from Xhosaland who had come to look at the new way in which Xhosa people were living in the place of the Rhanugas, and who, as they travelled, bought land for them and built schools. They said that they, too, had land that they were prepared to forfeit; land not far from here and a short distance from the sea. We promised them that we were willing to respond to them, and that we had heard them. Indeed, we had heard them.

At sunrise the following day it was obvious that a large meeting was to be held. It was widely announced up to the borders and across the rivers and beyond. The team from the town of Zathuza was aligned with the Manyano, the Union of Young Men, and was well represented, dedicated to being involved in discussions and decisions. People who had not been expected arrived in a hurry and out of breath, without any of us even knowing that they were aware of the meeting. Many people came on foot and horseback.

After breakfast the meeting started, and the biggest venue in that area was packed to full capacity. Not a single issue caused division, as the atmosphere was one of unity; it was what we had become accustomed to during our travels: all desiring or already busy building schools, buying land, and teaching different academic and handwork studies.

The first item on the agenda was whether a subject could be debated by both the Union of Young Men and the Union of Women. The issue of land was intensively discussed; in particular, land leading to a harbour was a top priority; so was the advancement of physical exercise for young men. We learnt that some places did not even have the beginning of education or buildings. Then suddenly somebody said, "We look like over-ambitious people if we discuss so many subjects without tabling anything." This voice was heard and listened to; men were eager to become involved and it was clear that for serious discussion to take place, things had to be put on an agenda.

This broke the silence! The urge to discuss in depth became obvious: after a man had said something, he would realise that he had not said it thoroughly enough, and then start again. A person who gave six oxen would later feel that he had done nothing, and fetch two more oxen and their yokes. During this period, valuable cattle were donated. Men brought tens and tens of bags of wheat, maize and beans, and a man was unashamed to leave his kraal empty.

The bell for lunchtime rang and rang, but the meeting was bursting with determination which had grown into a spirit of activism. People were saying they were fighting darkness and they wanted light; if these cattle of theirs could assist in that battle, they should help, and they were offering them. It was difficult to break for lunch after these heated debates, and before the second session resumed, the house was already full, with everyone urging the session to begin. First was a certain man who came from his employer and brought the little money that he had asked him to keep aside, and he poured in £200. The next one said: every hundred that we allow to be kept for us by the settlers makes us unfit for this endeavour, and he poured in £400; a man following them said that foreign metals were not compatible with our vision – something walking on its feet was more befitting, and then left his wagon and its yoke with twelve oxen. People incited one another: pay!

Late in the day, the men had no more to donate; their supply was exhausted. A man sitting in front, a man from the Tshawe clan, Tokazi's father, started counting and announced that the money on the table that day amounted to £10 500. Before the meeting was adjourned until the following morning, three men gratefully poured out their warm thanks to the Creator of all things.

The meeting started again the following day. Some had not been present the previous day, while others were still giving offerings that led to another £500, so now they could talk about an amount of over £10 500. It also emerged that the two farms near the sea could be acquired easily, and there would still be money left over. Nevertheless, the meeting was in favour of borrowing a small amount from the local chief of the Tshawe clan, Tokazi's father, so that they could speak to the Union of Young Men, the government, and the town council on the strength of it. And so it happened – the chief lent them another £11 000 to bring the total to £22 000 from Mnandi.

On the third day, the meeting started with the reading of a letter from the government, offering assistance to a school in Mgudu and another one at Zuba, and promising to contribute the same amount that had been put on the table by the people. A letter from the council of Zathuza expressed pride in our deliberations, and pledged assistance throughout the project, as well as a contribution equalling whatever people put up. A decision was accepted that we should also join the Union of Young Men that had been launched in town, contributing an amount of £22 000 to them to help with projects earmarked for implementation.

When the Union of Young Men heard about the Mnandi decision – its members were represented in large numbers here – it announced an immediate interim meeting, because the strongest advocacy indeed came from these men from Xhosa-land, so it would be futile to discuss this matter after they were already preparing to leave. The meeting took place at Mnandi and the following decisions were accepted:

1. The fact that the Union is to have a branch here at its home is welcomed, but the area it covers should begin at the sea and stretch to a big city like Zathuza.
2. All the money collected here will be used for local projects, and local branches will also do likewise. And everyone will be compensated according to his offering.
3. The two farms near Mnandi beach have been acquired. Two farms at Siganga are also taken.
4. A high school building should be built as well as a gym that should be run intensively, and guns should be available if possible.
5. Studies of medicinal trees are very necessary and should commence, and those trees should be intensively planted in fields earmarked for that purpose. Men with medicines for cattle should come forward; medicines for healing broken

bones should also be presented; and men specialising in various human ailments should come forward. Houses for purifying and mixing these medicines should be built and operated like chemists.

6. Builders of sea vessels and carriages for travelling on the beach up to the sea are sought from the outset. Diggers of cement-lined storage spaces should start working to store thousands and thousands of sacks of food so they will remain fresh for many years.

7. Agriculture: the establishment should house the following: draughtsmen of house plans; pounders of steel and those who can smelt metals; makers of clay dishes; cleaners of sheep wool and those who can comb, spin and weave it; planters of cotton, linen and producers of silk; shoemakers; various kinds of machines that local learners will be taught to use; and those familiar with making fire by rubbing uluzi sticks against uzwathi sticks in the old way; the indescribably beautiful things made of imizi and injica, basket grass, – with which ornaments for the arms and ankles are made.

8. Surveying of a site at Siganga has already started, construction has followed and the hotel is at an advanced stage. Control of the sites should be entrusted to the Union of Young Men, and it should do the advertising for the tourist house. Sites have been surveyed, and the angles of the Mnandi harbour should also be surveyed so that construction can begin.

9. Another significant item that needs to be started at Zathuza is a printing press; the town has given them its printing press so that printing can begin although the building is still under construction.

10. Another item that cannot be left out is that a store room should be opened immediately at Zathuza with a branch at

Mnandi, and through its distribution have branches all over the country.

These resolutions were taken at the meeting held at Mnandi with the Union of Young Men, and they were sent to the town council for approval, and for support for the items that they could support; the same was sent to the government. An agreed-upon committee was appointed to advance these resolutions, to leave none of them unattended, and to implement everything as soon as possible.

12

Revival and conclusion

After this meeting, the remaining issues were suspended, and revival services to strengthen and spread the Word took place in the area from the town to Zuba and Mgudu, as far as Mnandi. People were admitting their sins and repenting, but the group from Xhosaland was somewhat disjointed and scattered. One day during a big revival service held at Mgudu on the day of the Lord, an old man raised his voice, confessing that he had been a murderer of people all his life. Killing was familiar to him; he had also been present when two criminals were shot by a white man when they tried to attack him by surprise in the dense forest of Mgudu. He revealed many other events he had been part of – when some of his companions were arrested and hanged, but he repeatedly escaped. He described in detail a certain day back in the past, when they were going to attack a visitor in the densest part of a forest, but were held back by a Lawu person, who then fell ill with a stomach ache and died. The man then turned to me and said he recognised me; today he was casting away his past behaviour, and by the grace of God he wanted to live for Him, although he was far advanced in age.

At this juncture the visitors decided it was time to return home to Xhosaland, but it was clear that not all of them could leave because of the work that had emerged in this new country. Three men of our area were identified as being fit for the projects that had been started, so as not to leave them unattended. For them, going back home meant that they then had to prepare their belongings, arrange domestic matters, and come back to be members of the Rhanuga people. This matter was agreed upon in good faith; and although we of Xhosaland were sad to lose such men, we understood how needed they were in that central land, Mnandi.

That was what my second visit to my aunt's place at Mnandi was like. We were happy to be there, and the event was so remarkable that one could be excused for assuming that important theological schools had supported it. But that was not the case: it simply had the support that a nation gives its citizens. It had the enthusiasm of the people, and, as the Bible says, "For whoever wants to save their own life will lose it, but whoever loses his life for my sake will save it." (Luke 9:24)

When we were back at home in Xhosaland, news came frequently from the Mnandi region, and it was good news. It was evident that progress was firm and that education had become deeply rooted and its standard was high. The reader will understand why it was that experts from Japan, Scotland and England, America, Germany, Italy, and Abyssinia visited there, as well as those from our own country. Their visits were possible because commercial ships travelled to nearby harbours. It was said that the poverty that used to exist in that area was now non-existent. It was also said that people shared as others arrived there one by one; there was vast wealth there, and the men who had originally found that place completely deserted and had had to plan their projects from scratch, were now forgetting the deficiencies of those early days. And let me not talk about the clothes from there: they were recognised by everyone. It would take more time than I have to give details of the various projects and important events, but they can be picked up in the newspapers from those places.

I need to pause for today; if I get an opportunity to return to that region, I will go, and come back and tell you what I have seen and heard. It is said that independent governance has been established in that new country; it is under the control of the same government as we have – but the qualities of the place are boundless. For now,

GOODBYE!

Don Jadu

SECTION THREE

The waking up of black people in accordance with their tradition

INTRODUCTION

This page has been prepared to introduce the third part of the novelette entitled *Don Jadu* that has already been well read in its first two parts, published three years ago.

I am sending this part to a writers' competition: the May Esther Bedford Prize[7].

It is written in the new isiXhosa orthography.

SE Krune Mqhayi
Hill of Glory
Berlin, Cape Province
August 1935

THE CHALLENGE!

There is an important narrative these days that states: the black man should get off the back of the white man and be independent and succeed on his own, in accordance with the traditions and customs of his origin; and he should stop frequently emulating the whites, whose livelihood is different from his.

Black men accept this narrative, and also the challenge. They accept it, saying, "Give us space, and refrain from being a barricade and a bar of steel or wood that keeps restraining us when we want to advance ourselves."

The start of this endeavour was the country of Mnandi with which we set an example.

13

The great country of magical change

For whoever wants to save their own life will lose it, but whoever loses their life for my sake will save it. Luke 9:24

Even though we went back home, it was as if we were still in the country of Mnandi, because of how we had been cared for, and how we, too, cared for that new country.

Indeed, our team of fellow men who came home with us after they had already found jobs in that new country did not take long to act: they announced to the white and black houses of government that they were departing as they were needed in Mnandi.

The houses of chiefs, headmen and people gathered, and it was clear that the team had to be allowed to go freely and in good spirits so that their journey could be pleasant and their work successful.

These men were instructed thoroughly about the things they should do as men of the nation: to have respect and pride, to be considerate and imaginative, and to establish chiefs in whom they could take pride themselves, as well as in their own nation.

They promised never to forget their home, this very one, and that in everything they did there, they would always try as best they could to ensure that it remained aligned with this home.

The magistrates instructed them emphatically that they should not do things in haste and without thinking carefully.

They should be on good terms with one another, and they added, "We are talking like this because of the rumours that are heard, that the new country is to be tested in how it will control its affairs in accordance with the traditions and rules of your origins, enhanced through its national lineage and with the government serving as protector of that nation. You, the men of Xhosaland, are asked to be leaders and advisers in such matters; the responsibility will be upon your shoulders. Go, and have a pleasant journey!"

Before the men were allowed to leave, food was prepared at the chiefs' homesteads; cattle and sheep and goats were slaughtered, delights ensued, and speeches were delivered giving advice about looking after one another. The nation was joyful – the older people and the youth as well as the younger ones.

This was concluded by ministers of various denominations through great revival services and blessings; and that was the end. They tied up their belongings, loaded them, and driving their chosen livestock, they left with many family members and other people in their care.

The names of the three men who left need to be known in this section:

1. *Jiya Sogoni:* – This man was well educated, although not rich, and he was still young.
2. *Bell Zilo:* – He was a town boy, familiar with the attractions of towns, and who had experience of meetings with both white and black people. He was also not very rich.
3. *Gosa Sontonga:* – This was a man who owned things and was rich in some ways; a farmer of high esteem, farming mainly with crops on big paid-off tracts of land.

We have already indicated that these men were of good character and religious.

Indeed, when these men arrived in their new country, they chose places suitable for advancing the projects and the people who lived there. In various places they established Eyes-of-the-Nation, with annual national gatherings where various individuals summoned by their countries to attend were present. They established strong agriculture and livestock farming groups; although these had not existed previously, the arrival of these men advanced them immensely. They established Christian Unions for women, for men, and for the youth, and revived those that were on the brink of collapse. They established a Board of the House, which had to look at the state of the buildings and the maintenance of the establishment, and its co-operation with other nations, people, and languages.

Education was declared compulsory and every effort was made to make it available. Aquatic education was introduced: ship-building was taught, and a group of young men was put together to live on or near the sea, studying it and piloting the ships and boats. And truly, within a few years, businesses were growing. Softening and tanning of hides, and combing, twisting and braiding of wool were substantial occupations. Properly tilled land was prepared for cotton plantations, and the cotton was used for making clothes, although there were rumours that there was another cotton project that the government had approved.

Experts from different countries and various groups that had been recruited came with their own machines to fast-track these projects. There was no longer only one newspaper; through wide support several were published daily; they had been made the most of, and became substantial newspapers that were useful in terms of teaching and support.

This nation of Mnandi was based on deep and solid foundations, similar to those of the bigger country. Its citizens were diligent and became aware of their rights and those of the nation they belonged to; they sought understanding and wisdom, and the well-being of people and that of their livestock; and they embraced their nationality, their language, and the service of the Bible.

Above all, they had that most scarce of qualities, even in the strongest nations: unity and co-operation.

14

Self-governance

I have not come to do away with them, but to make their teachings come true. Matthew 5:17

Because of the good progress made in this country, the authorities in government wanted the place to be part of a trial, a testing ground, and to investigate whether what had been talked about was true, namely that the black nation had the ability to manage its affairs conscientiously and successfully – because indeed, in their origins, they were people who had always governed themselves.

The goal they strove for was to advance themselves through their customs and traditions. They tried to lessen the influence of white customs that were threatening to overwhelm them, and that even caused various diseases whose origins were unknown, as well as much poverty and suffering that were uncalled for. It was on account of these problems that many liars had emerged among the nation, as well as loafers and those who desert their households and their families, their wives and children.

This matter of self-governance had, however, been spoken about before by the magistrates. It was then tabled in Parliament in Cape Town, and having followed the protocol, became the focus of a discussion as to whether the country of Mnandi should be allowed to govern itself and to control the affairs of its nation, with the people taxing themselves and controlling their finances and all that was theirs. The colonial government would just offer a wing of security and investigate matters that might be a danger to the Mnandi nation. The suggestions were submitted to Parliament and were passed easily, as they did not have much opposition.

Mnandi's type of government was seen as being the same as that of the Judges in the Holy Bible: that is to say, there should be an election, and a particular individual had to be installed in power for some years, even if he was somebody who had been elected before; a person could be re-elected if he did satisfactorily and if nobody else was a better contender. The colonial government did not stipulate a resolution, and said that the nation should stipulate its own laws for its own government or control.

Eventually it was seen that details of this successful discussion in Parliament should be sent back to the nation of Mnandi. The first thing that was done was that the Parliamentary Committee tasked to handle this matter called some of the leaders of the Mnandi community one by one, trying to get the opinions of Mnandi citizens themselves. But the leaders were unanimous, did not argue, and had the same opinion as the citizens. This helped the committee a lot in its work, making it easy.

It became clear to the parliament of the larger country that this success story should be reported to Britain, to be approved there, and the findings concerning the endeavour should be understood there as well. The British Parliament embraced this story with enthusiasm and also announced that it wished to observe the endeavour itself and to see the Mnandi nation. This happened thanks to good co-operation with the people on both sides of the Kei River.

In size, Mnandi, that was to have its own government, was the same as the area that was later called the Transkei Territory[8]. Its government had to be the same size as the Great Council, which meant it should have the same number of magisterial towns. When the population was counted, it was found that the number of people in Mnandi was double that of the Transkei Territory, and so were the incoming finances.

The finances were a sore point in Parliament. One group asked: "So is it a sin to trust black people with so much money?" and they were not shaken from this viewpoint. Another group said that even if the experiment was executed, as far as finances were concerned, there should be a limit – which meant that a team of white people would handle and control it for them, even if it was just for a few years, until they learnt to handle it on their own. But this group was massively defeated by the majority in Parliament.

There were as many nations in that new country as there were in the Cape Province at that time. It was clear that the language of the Mnandi government had to be isiXhosa; there were only a few members of other nations who could have made a claim for their languages. Because the English language was the language of the colonial government, it should, anyway, also be intensively taught – as its claim in this new government was obvious.

The government in control voiced the following: "The people who are given the right to handle their governance through their original traditions and customs will try to develop protocols and laws in the manner derived from their origin; but that does not mean that they should cast away what is beneficial to them, simply because it is from white people."

The ultimate goal was stated thus: acceptance of the Word and of progress are not reasons for casting off traditions and customs that are central to the nation's existence; on the contrary, they should assist the nation in living a fulfilled life. That means they are to be practised in ways that accord with our traditions, and if they advantage our people. Their purpose will then be felt in the blood, heart and mind of a human being. There was also a point of view that not everything in our traditions is wholesome; some things are done merely because they are the custom, but without offering anything that is truly healthy to people.

Likewise, concerning white people, there were many things that helped us when they came, and that we revived through them and woke up to, where we had been drowning and drowning from lack of strength and determination in body and mind.

On account of these facts, it became clear that the traditional reign of chiefs as it was, would not be appropriate; the type of rule that seemed to be helpful would be to allow people of high esteem to take up vacant positions – especially if they had wide knowledge of Xhosa culture. They should also be individuals who loved and respected the government of Britain. In short, it was clear that the authorities would be men who were well versed on both sides – in isiXhosa and English.

15

Dondolo

Why do you ask my name in spite of its prominence? Judges 12:18

At this point, the colonial government tried its best to find a man who seemed to be suitable for this position; this was particularly important as he was to establish something that had not been there before. Opinions on this matter were asked by the Parliamentary Committee of all the leaders of this land who were invited; and it happened that they all elected the same person, each giving his own opinion without having met to discuss it at all. That one person that they agreed on was Don Jadu.

The powers that be were not aware of this elected man; they did not know of him. Even more importantly: he didn't come from their area, but from far away in Xhosaland. When they consulted women, it was clear that they understood this man well, and his roots also. It was then obvious that they should ask him to start and establish this new nation and all that it entailed.

Citizens of Mnandi told the government the following: "Do not think that the person we are talking about is a foreigner from a far-away country who does not understand the matters of this new nation. We say that he knows more than we who are here, and whatever you see us to be is of his doing; therefore we consider him to be the establisher of this place and this nation, because without him, we were not even known in the outside world, and we, too, knew nothing about it. Furthermore, he is already an honoured and respected man throughout this nation, and he is well versed in English and isiXhosa, knowing the narratives, customs and traditions."

The discussion ended there, and Dondolo, the son of Jadu, was elected unanimously and with mutual agreement, to become the first president of the country of Mnandi.

Mnandi was originally the name of the most advanced area in this region, an area near the sea in the valley of the Mnandi River. But this name was now bestowed on the new country, as the house did not agree to the name, emaRhanugeni (meaning "at the Rhanugas"). Some thought that the name emaRhanugeni was insulting and humiliating, because it implied moving and settling elsewhere for work, while the land of Mnandi had belonged to their fathers and their chiefs before, and they therefore could not be humiliated as newcomers, because they had actually *preserved* the land. Some even said that the word "Rhanuga" was not isiXhosa but a loanword, therefore it did not suit their country at all.

To say that Mnandi was a country in the centre – or to call it the Central Area – was because it was indeed in the centre, between the east and the west. The language of the people there was very mixed with languages of others from their countries – coloured people, the Qwelane clan, Boers, and the remainder of the Bushmen; but at this time the people remembered their original language, isiXhosa, very well; they specifically wanted it to be revived intensively along with their customs and traditions. That is why to them a person who was actually from Xhosaland could not fail or lose his way – and the fact that some from outside were already referring to Mnandi as "Kaffirland" simply strengthened their resolve, their determination.

Dondolo said he was still too shy to talk about himself; but, like Nehemiah of the Bible and other authors, he felt compelled to do so, not through praises, but by delivering a speech.

He said the first thing he wanted to remark upon was that he had no time to respond to the constant stream of letters from his friends, telling him that they had heard about the discussions, and they had also seen news in newspapers, but they did not know that the people of this land were planning that *he* should be the one to start and establish that nation. He had answered none of those letters, he said.

Ultimately a letter from the council arrived, and it was written by the secretary and the chairperson of the council. The letter was not asking, but informing him that a leadership position was coming to him, and he should therefore not be surprised by it.

"When this declaration arrived, it was at a time that I was very involved in chieftaincy matters in Xhosaland," says Dondolo. "At that point, the Xhosa nation was dealing with issues that affected them intensely; news to do with chieftaincy was highly prioritised, and their lineage of relatives, their areas of chieftaincy, and land were among those matters, because the state was finally in favour of giving the chiefs some status. Some heirs whose younger brothers had taken over were investigated. Some said that because they had fought, they were pulled down, and those who were good for nothing were elevated; some had been Unbelievers in Nongqawuse's time[9] and been stingy, refusing to kill their cattle, yet they were elevated and given the status of their older brothers who were then perceived as being the weaklings. Those matters needed constant work, and I could talk about them until dawn. As I am assumed to be a knowledgeable man about these matters and about the ways of the whites, all the chiefs and sub-chiefs wanted my voice regarding them. I therefore had no opportunity to concentrate on external matters at all.

"Eventually a letter from Mnandi arrived, written by the writers of the initial letter from the council, and it was clearly a request to come to that country, as I was a person who had already brought about progress. This letter did not give me room to answer, because, even while asking me, it also indicated that they were coming to talk to me in person about this matter.

"I informed the people and chiefs with me about the content of this letter, and each one gasped. Some answered, 'Is there anyone who would leave his home in these trying times and go to the land of people who have left Xhosaland and settled on farms as labourers, as amaRhanuga?' The answer to that became important, and it was the talk of everyone, around fireplaces and in households, and among the nation as a whole. When news of this topic spread widely and people were talking about it, some said that they knew I would not agree to leave the chief and the nation here. Some were saying: 'Is there anyone who would leave his troubled home to go and live among the Rhanugas?' Others were saying, 'Don't you know that these Rhanugas will just go home when they are tired of being amaRhanuga, because they will have remembered their roots.' Some people were saying this, and others saying that, and no one was giving others a chance to talk.

"When they were at the peak of their altercation, seven men in horse-drawn wagons arrived, and they requested a meeting of the people and chiefs.

"The day of the meeting was set; most of the chiefs and their councillors were present, and women and ordinary people. Even two magistrates came uninvited to listen; they had just heard about this matter, as it was the talk among the people of the government, and they had obviously been told about what was happening and about the arrival of these men.

"The visitors arrived not at my place, but at the Great Place in whose jurisdiction I lived in Xhosaland. As they were not sure how they would be treated in this country, on account of the matter that brought them here, they came with a lot of provisions. Those provisions took time to finish, because in Xhosaland a visitor does not eat his own food once he is in this land. The Great Place slaughtered small livestock, to be followed by an ox.

"The day of the meeting arrived, and the men from the Central Area, Mnandi, talked and talked, having come themselves to beg for this gentleman, tabling their reasons and causes for asking him, knowing very well that he was busy. The Tshawe clan, however, dominated the talk and refused to accept anything that was out of order or irrelevant – they insisted that the issue should be dealt with, not as an emotional decision but as a private internal matter for the Tshawe.

"Absolutely nothing was referred to me; my opinion was not asked; I was not even recognised as having a say in whether I go or not, because the chiefs were in agreement – 'Let us recognise these men's requests, we must let Dondolo go.' I was like a girl sent for marriage.

"The honourable men continued: 'That is our land, those are our people, the one who is being asked is our man and he is asked by us; therefore where is the loss in this matter? Is all not a reward and a gain to us, and a right?'

"Those were the final words. The visitors were released with unusual kindness, being told, 'You must look out for the man at the next month-end.'

"Let me summarise by saying that my release was immediately marked by the divine services of honourable men and the entire nation; the ministry was present, people who praised the blessings I received. Instructions, rhetoric, greetings, the giving of gifts, all happened together, long before the agreed thirty days ended.

"From my side I have to admit that I did not feel any pain or relief; I did not experience any joy or sorrow; I was just muddled, and my body was tired! But I was preparing; my belongings were tied up and sent; then, at last, I began to feel relaxed and left."

16

Departure and inauguration

The emperor gave me all through the good hand of God.
Nehemiah 2:8

I do not want to tire readers of this book by giving them details and thoughts about my departure from my home in Xhosaland. In the previous chapter I mentioned the deliberations of the nations and the people, as well as those of church ministers and women, and the school families, in making introductions and giving instructions.

The chieftaincy gave me five households to take to the new country, I being a man of goodwill and who lived well with their families and their homesteads. Two of these households belonged to men of the Word; wise men when it comes to the Word, and they were also serious resisters of strong drink. Their families were properly taught in big schools, and they were well brought up at home.

Three of the households belonged to traditional men, although they were not using red ochre anymore. The three of them sent their children to school, and they directed and managed their households very well.

People do not get tired of talking about things that are far from them, but they quickly get tired of talking about things that are *not* far from them, that are on their shoulders only. This matter of being given these five households became the talk of the nation, with people asking one another what was happening here. Was chieftaincy being forced on me? Even if I was awarded a chieftaincy, how big could it be that it deserved five households! Isn't it true that the leadership of a nation comprises two people: the prime minister and his deputy?

The honourable men did not entertain any of these qualms. They decided that they knew exactly what they were doing: taking an ember of one fireplace to ignite another one. These households were chosen from various clans, so that each man could be the eye of his clan, and the things that the clan members found healthy, they could take back to their erstwhile chiefs.

In addition to these five households, there was another group that desperately wanted to follow, but there was no agreement on their migration. Some of them satisfied themselves then by simply accompanying us, saying that they would consider coming to us in the future.

The journey was not long, but it was slow. This immigration was widely known about in all the areas on the way, and it prompted wonderful kindness and hospitality that sometimes delayed us for a whole week. People came to the road in droves, and when we were near Mnandi, even those from there came out to meet us and show their appreciation to us. Eventually we reached Mnandi as a large crowd of people. Everything was deliberated in a just and proper way: we were put in our places, and all the people there and from afar prepared the welcoming with great cheerfulness and joy. People also came from other far-away areas to see for themselves if it was true that their prayers had been fulfilled, and that the president had come – because that position was named as such.

When we left home there were some magistrates who were attracted to all the deliberations accompanying my journey to Mnandi in the Central Area; it was their benevolence that drew them, and they desired only the success of the event. The magistrates said that this would have a positive influence on their part, and on their teachings to black people; they prided themselves on it, and of course did not wish their pride to fall.

They presented a speech to the meeting they hosted with chiefs and the people, and made the following point: "Today, this is the experiment that the government will drive, even spreading it to you from other countries if it succeeds." They advised the chiefs each to nominate a person to be their eyes and ears in that country, and that the chiefs should not take education of their sons and daughters lightly.

The government of the Union[10] also extended a hand of friendship and co-operation, dedicating itself to support Mnandi's new government with all its might as the heir it had given birth to, because the British government saw it in this way. It was very good that Great Britain gave its consent and would assist with governance.

The government sent gifts directly to me; it had already sent blessed gifts and good wishes to Mnandi. This support from many places became an important issue throughout the entire nation. It was discussed and spoken about in newspapers and social gatherings, and in other countries of other groups. It was criticised and praised, as is anything that is newly introduced, some seeing a lot of negative things, others seeing the whole thing as a mistake, even saying that they would not have said anything if this right had been given to other tribes, rather than the amaXhosa.

Eventually the day earmarked for the welcoming of the president arrived – and that became one long pleasurable event starting at mid-morning and continuing right through the night and to the next morning, with the citizens of Mnandi making their own entertainment, and enjoying songs and food. The ceremony was opened by the Governor-General, who cheerfully executed all the delicacies linked to that, and gave instructions in the name of the king and the British kingdom. He also addressed the nation: "The success of this undertaking does not solely lie on the shoulders of this president, but it also depends on each one of you abiding by this government's authority together, no matter whether you are happy, pained, busy, or whatever; rules must be complied with, and there should be no underestimation of the magistrates, the police, and whatever exists under the sovereignty of this state. You must understand that if you destroy this, you are also destroying most of your nation."

The servant of the kingdom continued, "Here is the land, you must make it give you good produce; do not rely on food from other countries; you have here a big country that is beautiful and that has rivers and water. Here are forests with large trees, and you also have the opportunity to plant more forests that you could use in building and construction. You will understand that no country is beautiful when it is parched or barren and has become bare, and when rain is scarce. As I mention this, I hear people say that people of your nation are skilled in handling an axe, but lack skill in planting. You must know that finance for sustaining it and for advocating for your government will come from you, except for some money for development; and be aware that people hate giving money to maintain their government – you must be aware of that, it is a disease, yes, a terrible disease. You must give your pledges with joy; this country and this endeavour should not fall apart, as this is an undertaking that has come to fruition despite its enemies; you must therefore not give them ammunition for criticising you, for taking advantage of you, for censoring you, or for whatever.

"If you multiply and become crowded, and find the land too small for you, do not cry, because all nations face the same problem; the only thing that you should do is to use the land that you have fruitfully. Let me be clear, people of Mnandi, that when talking about land, it is not only the surface that counts – the size of the country, the beauty, but also the wealth in the ground under your feet – be aware of that too.

"You, the President!" he continued, "I congratulate you for being in this high position among people from your tribe, and even though you are as high as this, it is also a very humble position. I hear that this nation nominated you unanimously, and you were not here, you were at your home in Xhosaland. This does not mean that they will always be unanimous, especially during projects carried out with little hope of success, and very hard, difficult programmes that discard most of the familiar traditional customs and adopt new ones. But this must be clear to you, President, and to anyone listening to me, that the whole world is looking up to you to become successful by virtue of your own nationality.

"You are at liberty to choose your own education, clothing, food, livelihood – but others must act in accordance with your traditional protocol; also, be on good terms with other tribes and nations and speakers of other languages, and work together with them, and borrow things from them that will be beneficial to you, and heal your people with them; they, too, will borrow many things from you that they find useful to themselves. You must preserve your unity, dedication and education, and the Word, as it is because of those things that today you have reached the level at which you can steer this ship with your own hands.

"On behalf of Great Britain and under the signatory of his Majesty the King of England and its colonies, through the powers and the authority vested in me, I am handing over this country and this nation to rule its own state under the protection of Britain. *May God bless the King.*"

17

Laws and codes of practice

Instead, new wine must be poured into fresh wineskins and the two must be preserved. Luke 5:38.

Even during the first gathering of the nation of Mnandi, laws and codes of practice such as the following were created, and it was said that they would be revisited regularly until they were refined and suited the people they were meant for, and those that hindered progress would be set aside:

1. *Religion.* – It is well known that Xhosa people are worshippers of the Creator, the Ever Present, the living God, although they worship Him through respect, by going to Him through their ancestors, their nationality and their clans. Today it is crystal clear that God is in three forms that make one God. One of these forms is the Son who came to make Himself the heir of the ancestors, where they all meet. Therefore today, entering God's territory is a right. The whole state is therefore under the Christian religion. The Holy Bible is the Word and contains God's laws.

2. *Governance.* – Anyone who knows Xhosa people will be aware that they are people who live with governance or rule throughout their lives; without reign or governance a Xhosa person has no life. Therefore the president here is in the place

of all chieftaincy, and everyone must kneel down before him. At a level below the president will be the head of state who presides over the Great Council; members of the Great Council come every year from the district councils, and the number of districts is thirty (30). Magistrates (black men) of those districts are the eyes and ears of the Honourable President in their districts – just like the rulers of hillsides and wilderness who rule for the Honourable King, passing judgements in some cases, and correcting society's way of life so that it is a good one.

3. *Term of the president.* – The president will be elected for five years; if he still pleases the people he will be re-elected, and he can be nominated again for a third term if he still pleases. But he will not be re-elected after fifteen (15) years, no matter how young he may be, and no matter how he pleases the nation. But at this time, there is a decree that the nation can go abroad to the king's palace, to ask for permission for five additional years.

4. *Household discipline.* – Every man who is the head of a household is accountable for any bad thing happening in his household, just as the glory is upon him for everything good and right that takes place in his household. Therefore the law from the Great Place is directed at him, and he must ensure that his whole family complies with it. Children are to listen to their mothers; mothers to listen to their children's fathers; fathers to listen to the chief; and the chiefs to listen to God.

5. *Education.* – The state and the clergy will work together as far as education is concerned. It will be compulsory in places that have the means to enforce it. It will be the prerogative of members of district councils to look out for families that do not get education because the parents are too poor to afford it, and to produce a report of such a matter

to the Council. The clergy has that prerogative too. A man who is overpowered by his child's refusal to go to school must report that matter as soon as possible to a minister of religion or to the member of the Council.

6. *Inkundla: the area between the cattle kraal and homestead.* – It is well known that Xhosa people perform all their holy ceremonies in the inkundla. Weddings, instructing of boys from the circumcision lodge, sacrifices and offerings and many other ceremonies are performed there. It is also a burial place for members of the household. Today temples appropriate for performing these ceremonies have been built – and suddenly inkundla is no longer holy for anything. Even though the state is of the Christian religion, it should not concern itself with sacrifices made for ancestors, and sacrifices of animal blood.

7. *Girls.* – Bringing up and grooming girls from childhood until marriage is the ultimate responsibility of women, led by the wife of the mfundisi – the minister of religion – and of the district magistrate. Among the Xhosa people there is a tradition that marks the reaching of puberty by a girl (ukuthomba). This tradition will not totally fade away over time, but the matter rests on the shoulders of the wife of the minister of religion and the wife of the district magistrate. The well-loved tradition among Xhosa people of examining a girl to see if she is still a virgin should not be practised, except when a particular girl's behaviour is doubted; that will have to be understood by the female traditional healer.

8. *Circumcision and initiation.* – It will be the duty of the minister of religion and the district magistrate to see to it that a baby boy is circumcised before the end of the month in which he was born. Baptism and circumcision must be done at the same time. After a period of fifteen to twenty

years, those boys must assemble in the temple. Food must be prepared for them, instructions will be given to them and gifts will be given to them; and the clergy must put their hands on them; the magistrate must be present as the eye of the Great Place. After that everyone will know that as of today these are men.

9. *Support of officials.* – Maintenance of the ministers of religion, like that of magistrates and teachers, comes from the Great Place. Congregations present their offerings and pay taxes at the same time. There is no differentiation between the policeman, the elder, the deacon and the minister of religion.

10. *Marriage.* – The value of marriage among Xhosa people is enormous. No matter whether other kinds of marriages are practised that include ceremonies such as oomiguqo – ritual kneeling – or drinking of amasi, sour milk, and no matter whether there is lobola, as there is among Xhosa people, there is only one truth: the truth that the service of marriage is above all those things and not in contrast with them. The minister of religion and the magistrate maintain the principles of marriage. Before a young man is allowed to get married, this man must understand how he is going to care for his wife. In all holy marriages, the marriage counsellor is the magistrate, and the minister of religion is the one who blesses. All marriages have documented reports in the magistrate's office and with the minister of religion; not one is transferred anywhere. Marriage is something that is never broken.

11. *Punishment.* – In Xhosa rule in the past, prison was never mentioned among punishments. Even today in this new small country, there is to be little use of it; because if punishment fails, offenders will then be directed by the rule of the Great Place.

i. A girl who misleads women and is seen to be pregnant must marry the young man responsible; but before marrying the young man, she will undergo a punishment called ukunqazela (meaning "be astonished at"); the young man will also have that punishment. This punishment is like this: there will be older men with grim faces, twenty of them, called to the temple to enter and sit there. The girl will be made to enter and stand in front of them for some time, while they look at her in silence. In the other room the young man will be looked at by twenty women with sombre faces. This punishment is very painful to young people.

ii. A woman who is found with another man, though she has her own, will remain in her marriage household, no matter how much her husband despises her. The other man will have to pay. There will be a feast at a social gathering place where there will be elder men and elder women. The first person to eat at that feast will be that woman, and she will eat alone and be witnessed.

iii. A man who kills a lover of his wife and a man who kills a person roaming about his homestead at night is not guilty of murder; however, according to the law, for three years, he will have to report at the Great Place every three months.

iv. A young man who has a wife and who impregnates a girl, whether this is his first offence or a repeat offence, will be sent away by train with his family to a faraway region and become a guard of wildlife for the Great Place there, even if it is in the forests. This will be for seven years, but he will be compensated. After serving those years he can decide where to go. If he repeats the same vice, he will go back to the wilderness and stay there for the rest of his life, but get adequate compensation for his job.

v. A thief must pay double the value of what he stole, as well as the costs of the proceedings of his case. If he steals again, he must repay the value four times. If he repeats this a third time, he must be sent away with his family to do work for the Great Place, guarding dams in the mountains; he will be adequately compensated, but half of his compensation for ten years will be deducted for the building of prisons.

vi. A person who deliberately persecutes another maliciously and spitefully must be sentenced to live for only ten days. A person who kills another while fighting must go away with his family and become a trainer of horses and donkeys belonging to the Great Place for five years. One who kills a person unintentionally must work for a whole year on machines threshing mealies, wheat, etcetera. All these individuals will get an adequate salary wherever they are.

vii. A man who owns a field of one acre is expected to produce a harvest of two bags per year, or make a profit of a specific amount. If the man fails to produce the number of bags, the state must take over the field for a year. The state then must give the man the profits. It should then give him back his field and assist him to prepare it. If he repeats the laziness, the field must again be sown by the state and he receives the dividends. Everything concerning fields is handled this way.

viii. There is no prohibition on the drinking of utywala, traditional beer; a person drinks it voluntarily, it being made at his household by his family, but he must not even think of selling it. In addition, shop owners must never sell malt liquor. Liquor from liquor shops is not allowed in these territories at all, but a person may make his own liquor of grapes that he grows in his own country, though he may not sell it.

ix. A person who is found blind drunk must be carried to a psychiatric hospital as he is also psychotic. He has to stay there for a week and be treated like a psychiatric patient, wearing the same clothing as other psychiatric patients. If he repeats the same behaviour, he must stay at the psychiatric hospital for a month. A person who is just drunk, makes a noise, interferes and does other related things, must also be treated like one who has collapsed from drunkenness. If they are not healed, they must stay at the psychiatric hospital for life, or their job and their life must be at the psychiatric hospital, and they must be paid for the help they render.

x. Vices like incest have customarily been much despised in the Xhosa kingdom; even today it is so. People who constantly desire each other, knowing that they have the same blood, have to be married in an unholy marriage by the clergy, and then they will be chased to faraway places where they will work where wood is carved and medicines are sifted. They will stay there for twenty years and get an adequate salary.

A person who has been charged with rape will stay in the mountains together with his family (if he has a family), digging stone for building households for the Great House, offices and prisons.

Other vices that are carried out on four-legged animals bear the same punishments, in a harsher manner.

For the time being, the laws that are written must be enough. There are many codes of practice and laws concerned with living as a nation.

18

Development and conclusion

He succeeds in whatever he does. Psalms 1:3

Although these codes of practice were harsh and were not neat and simple, they fortunately played their role very well, and in the eyes of important modern nations, Mnandi developed and eventually became what it had been placed on trial for, as an experiment. Through my thoughts on this, I can say:

1. This beautiful system happened through the people's compliance with the colonial state, not only their own state, and also because of the respect they had for Britain.

2. We achieved that because of the assistance that was made available by the entire government of the Union; it indeed proved wrong what some people had feared, namely that black people (for example, Sothos, Swazis, Tswanas) would never achieve anything independently because the state did not want the success of black people. Everyone was grateful for the assistance of this government of unity through its suggestions, benefits and advocacy.

3. People themselves, living under these laws, found they were not too modernised, and were not suspicious of them.

4. There were many nations and tribes that came here from their own places, through their work, and some of them even became citizens voluntarily. Those who had been here for

a year had voting rights, and there was no discrimination against them on grounds of nationality, race or religion. Never did those people raise a word of discontent. They abided by the judgements of black magistrates and judges, despite some uncompromising severity at times.

I, the President, must acknowledge that the success of this place was achieved thanks to these points I have raised. I must also acknowledge that I never imagined how beautiful my life here would be. The respect I received was the same as that given to the king, who is of royal blood, like all kings.

I was elected three times (five years per period), for fifteen years, and by almost the same numbers each time. That led to a visit overseas to Britain to ask permission for a fourth term, and the Royal House there acknowledged the request. I thus remained the President for exactly twenty years.

I wish good life and success to the people of Mnandi.

May God bless the King!

Today in my old age I have returned home to Xhosaland. One person asked, "So why did you leave the country that you worked for for so long, to end your life here?" My answer was: "By coming back home, I show my wish for a good and pure agenda in the Central Country, Mnandi; because if I had remained there it would be like a scar caused by a wood-borer; and above all, it was always my wish that I and the remnants of my chiefs bury each other."

The endeavour in Mnandi to show that black people can succeed by themselves, and through their own customs, was highly praised by all civilised and well-developed countries.

This country had a rich tradition of agriculture, and people cultivated with diligence and patience, and this fed everyone among them. Fruit that came from this country was amazing, and that of the best grades was sold in major countries.

The amount of wheat coming from there was enormous. Some even compared it to Russia and Egypt. Not to mention maize and rye, and livestock, too, which were produced in large quantities. Its pigs became a leading example among other nations. This country also produced things that it had been assumed it did not have: firstly there was coal, then zinc and copper. When all those things emerged, they attracted all the nations of the world, as was their custom.

The rights to membership of our parliament (as the partnership of the councils of this country was called) were the same for all males who had reached the age of twenty. People from other nations were given a year in order to learn the system of this country, and after that they received the rights. That was to be of great benefit to the country – the bringing of suggestions from wise tribes, and their diligence as well as their wealth.

Females were not given those rights, not because they were not granted, but they themselves did not wish to have them because of the magnitude of their work at home. Even the few that cried for the rights of women in the state did not get supporters.

Within the short period in which this new nation had been established, it had an amazing number of people in it.

Young men of the Sea Defence Force alone numbered 50 000 and its support was entirely shouldered by Britain; Britain did that with great respect, having an affection for the calf it had given birth to and that had made such good progress. The National Defence Force had about 70 000 members on foot and on horseback, things that were new among the Xhosa people. Although they were active in all these things, they did not abandon their Xhosa nationality, which was something that they needed.

The health of the nation was also very good compared with health in the townships of cities in other countries, and in rural areas of other places. It provided the beautiful sight of crowds of children of all ages in schools, up to grown-up boys and girls. Food for feeding families was purely organic and natural, and people's clothes fitted in a healthy way, a way that did not cause problems in blood circulation, and this was acknowledged by doctors. It was also very rare to hear of any tooth problems among the young ones,or problems with eyes or ears. It was like the old way of Xhosa living. Tuberculosis and lung problems were almost eradicated.

Animal skins and sheep and goat wool were all handled by their owners. They brought in a lot of revenue and were widely embraced in other countries where they were sold. People of other nations fought one another in their rush to get these animal skins and wool of the Central Country. Beautiful clothes were made of the leather, not to mention shoes.

Cotton was sown in significant amounts, then combed, twisted and knitted, and was used a lot in fashionable clothes. Methods of using various types of machines and of making steel were learnt overseas, and eventually there were schools for teaching the skills of smelting and casting steel.

Several men went overseas to learn about trees for building ships and other sea vessels. When they came back they planted the trees and later made small boats, steam tugs, ships and steamers. They also worked assiduously, without a pause, building trains. Thanks to these achievements, Xhosa people were seen as a nation that is known by others; their rich language was appreciated, and they continued to trade and advance business.

Through mutual co-operation between this nation and the Union, Xhosa people were increasingly understood by other nations overseas – even by those who did not know the Xhosa. Through trading with bigger nations and through education, they restored the image from their forefathers' time of a nation with credibility, beauty, strength, intellect, truth, bravery, and self-control.

Eventually the British government merged the Sea Defence Force of this Central Country with its own navy, because the teaching was the same – and there was a lot that their young men would learn from the black men, just as the young black men would learn a lot from the white ones. That resulted in mutual goodwill, and it so happened that it would lead to some excellent and major developments.

As time passed, young black men led by young white men were able to go around the globe in steamers and ships built by themselves, wearing clothes made in Mnandi.

One of their most convincing achievements was their impact on black island nations that had been unbending in their refusal to welcome the Word and education: now that they saw these other black men, they started to understand that this was a worthwhile cause. That was how those nations were brought in.

Everything that had been on trial, before it was acknowledged, understood and verified as having succeeded, had to be evaluated. This endeavour also had the opportunity to be thoroughly judged, and was found to be solid. The reader will want to understand how it was thoroughly investigated, and with what. For that question the reader will have to excuse us when we answer with one voice, as the time is already exhausted, and say: During the war when Britain was surrounded by many nations, don't you remember the assistance – the food, clothes, timber – that came with Mnandi's army? Don't you remember that when those nations took their armies against those of Mnandi, the people of Mnandi stood together in unity for all those fifteen months? Most importantly, famine killed no one, no horses or dogs were eaten, and the plague of fever that prevailed during that period did not enter Mnandi. Traditional healers praised this, saying, "This nation was saved through its good behaviour."

The British king sent the Governor-General to be his mouthpiece to thank this nation, which, despite being so new, stood up tenaciously to help the fatherland in its time of distress – and so: became free.

During this last visit of the Empire Delegation, the government back in Britain requested that its members should not fail to visit Mnandi and continue to convey the gratitude of the king to this nation. In truth, that day became a significant one – for they were praising and encouraging this nation themselves, acknowledging that as from now, the Palace would see it as its right hand, and the most prominent tribe on whom to depend.

There is nothing to say about the visitors from faraway places and overseas countries who came to see this wonderful nation that had developed so quickly. They left utterly amazed, and, just as the Queen of Sheba said: "We were not told even the half!"

May God bless the King!

Notes

1 A "Rhanuga" was a person who had left their traditional Xhosa home to seek work on farms owned by whites, or in towns, sometimes settling there. The word is thought to have originated in the 1830s from *Ganna Hoek* in the Cradock district, a place-name that stood for several towns and farming regions where rural Xhosa people had moved in search of work, lost much of their traditional way of living and in some cases, intermarried. Some lost even their language, which was replaced by Afrikaans. Note that *rh* in isiXhosa is pronounced like *g* in Afrikaans.

2 The Xhosa chief Maqoma's people became known as the Jingqi people. The name was from Maqoma's ox, Jingqi, that used to wander as it wished, recognising the land as its own and going wherever it wanted.

3 This traditional make-up was mainly ochre, an earth-based pigment of different colours, but especially red.

4 Revival campaigns were (and still are) intended to revive Christian religious spirit among people. Revival services among the Xhosa may last all night, with singing and clapping, and several preachers taking it in turn to strengthen religious commitment in the congregation.

5 Mqhayi is playing on the similarity between the name of the Zima clan and the word *izim*, an ogre-like cannibal in folklore.

6 The school at St Matthews was part of a historic mission station, acclaimed as a centre of education for girls.

7 Mqhayi won the May Esther Bedford Competition for Bantu Literature for Part 3 in 1935; the competition was run under the auspices of London University.

8 The Transkei Territory included the districts of Butterworth, Dutywa, Centane, Ngqamakhwe, Tsomo and Willowvale; though geographically similar, it is not to be confused with the apartheid-era Bantustan named Transkei that was created in1963 (long after Mqhayi's death).

9 Nongqawuse (c. 1841–1898) was a young Xhosa woman whose prophecies led to the cattle-killing movement and famine of 1856–1857.

10 The Union of South Africa, formed in 1910.

Glossary

dompas a derogatory word for the pass or identity book that black men in South Africa had to carry

donga a gully, usually caused by soil erosion

erven (singular: **erf**) plots of land

Great Place the homestead or court of a Xhosa king or chief

inspan to harness oxen or horses in order to pull a wagon

Jere Got Don Jadu's version of Afrikaans "Here God" meaning Lord God

kaffir historically an extremely insulting term for black people

kameraad comrade (Afrikaans)

knobkierie a stick with a knob at one end, often used as a weapon

Lawu (sometimes considered derogatory) a Khoi person; a coloured person (of mixed race)

lobola traditionally cattle and other livestock paid by a bridegroom to the family of his future wife, to unify the two families

Manyano an organisation of people, from a word in isiXhosa meaning unity

mfundisi minister in the church

mfundisikazi female minister in the church

ochre people the Xhosa people, from the tradition of applying a type of red earth-based ochre to their clothing and bodies

oom uncle; also used to address an older man (Afrikaans)

Rhanuga (See note 1 on page 105)

Royal House the homestead or court of a Xhosa king

sjambok a long, stiff whip

ubuntu humaneness, kindness, compassion; linked to the expression "A person is a person through other people"

About the translators

Thokozile Mabeqa

Thokozile Mabeqa was born in Alice in the Eastern Cape in 1952. She is now retired but is still involved with academic work at the University of the Western Cape (UWC), where she has lectured on literature, cultural studies, translation, and editing both in English and isiXhosa. She has a Master's degree in translation studies from Stellenbosch University, and another Master's degree in oral literature from the University of the Western Cape. She began her teaching career in the Eastern Cape, then she moved to Cape Town to pursue the same career. Later she lectured in methods of teaching isiXhosa and school management at a college of education in Cape Town. She has also taught first-time learners of isiXhosa in her private capacity. She was involved in developing an isiXhosa communication curriculum at the Peninsula Technikon (now the Cape Peninsula University of Technology) before moving to UWC. Mabeqa has a wide range of translation experience, from academic texts to national government documents, and has also assisted the Stellenbosch University Language Centre.

Thenjiswa Ntwana

Thenjiswa Ntwana was born in Queenstown in the Eastern Cape in 1968. After training as a teacher, she taught Mathematics and Science at Chris Hani Secondary School in Khayelitsha, Cape Town, and then moved on to a lecturing post at the Cape Peninsula University of Technology (CPUT). She joined the isiXhosa Department at the University of the Western Cape (UWC) in 1995 and began teaching Xhosa studies, specialising in literature, culture, sociolinguistics and creative writing, among other fields. She graduated with a BA Honours degree in 1994 and a BEd (Bachelor of Education) degree in 1996 from UWC, and then completed an MPhil degree in Translation and Editing at Stellenbosch University in 2005. She is currently working towards a PhD degree in Translation at UWC.

Nosisi Mpolweni

Nosisi Mpolweni was born in Cape Town in 1954 and grew up moving between Cape Town and the Eastern Cape. She studied to become a teacher and taught at a primary school in Gugulethu before moving to the University of South Africa (UNISA) where she studied and also lectured, eventually becoming head of the isiXhosa Department. Mpolweni moved to the University of the Western Cape in 1996, where she taught isiXhosa. She has worked on a number of writing and translation projects for publishing houses, and has translated documents for the Department of Arts and Culture. She worked with Antjie Krog on the translation and writing of witnesses' testimonies during the Truth and Reconciliation Commission (TRC) hearings. She is currently a coordinator of an arts and crafts organisation in Gugulethu and works as a property consultant.

To view the translators speaking about the Africa Pulse series, visit
www.youtube.com/oxfordsouthernafrica